Don't forget to sign up for my spam-free newsletter at www.tlpayne.com to be among the first to know of new releases, giveaways, and special offers.

❀ Created with Vellum

Contents

Preface

Real real towns, cities, and institutions are used in this novel. However, the author has taken occasional liberties for the story's sake, and versions within these pages are purely fictional.

Thank you in advance for understanding an author's creative license.

ONE

Ayden Miller

New Eden Compound
Somerset Township
Washington County, Pennsylvania
Day Twenty-Two

Ayden Miller sat in a metal folding chair next to Clara's bed. With his elbows resting on his knees, he watched New Eden's medical team work with quiet efficiency. The medical bay of the compound was a functional, rectangular steel shipping container filled with the scent of surgical scrubbing solution and a hint of chlorine disinfectant. A mixture of low voices, the occasional clink of medical instruments, and the distant murmur of the compound going about its day swirled around him.

Inside the converted shipping container, the air conditioner battled to keep the temperature cool against the late summer heat outside. While giving him a tour of the compound, Laney pointed out the solar array that supplied power to the medical bay. Ayden was amazed by how prepared these guys were before the EMP attack. He felt almost safe behind the four-foot-wide walls surrounding the compound.

Beside him, Clara was dozing after receiving a herbal remedy to help her rest. Her mind and her body had been through hell over the last three weeks. Ayden had been concerned her leg might have permanent damage after she was shot back in New York City, but the compound's doctor had given her a good prognosis for a complete recovery.

Ayden turned his attention to Tyson Mueller. Lying on a portable examination table, the man winced as a nurse replaced the bandages on his arm and treated the burns on his back. Lines of pain were etched around his eyes as she worked, but his attention seemed fixed on something beyond the physical discomfort.

Serenity's father, Keith, the most severely injured patient, was receiving treatment from the compound's surgeon in the clinic's front room. The occasional low command of the doctor to an assistant or the soft beep of a monitor leaked through the thin partition.

As Ayden shifted in his chair, trying to find a more comfortable position, the sound of hushed voices caught his attention. Laney was telling her father about their experience at Camp Evergreen in Maryland.

"The security team at Evergreen didn't even see it coming, Dad," Laney said. "We were sleeping when the PLA hit us. It was… it was a massacre."

"Wasn't DaSilva in contact with US forces in the area?" Mueller asked, adjusting his pillows.

"No, their radios weren't working. There was some type of signal jamming from the PLA. From what we learned at Owen Graff's place, the PLA likely targeted Camp Evergreen because of their ham radio transmissions. I'm thinking when the Chinese forces saw their firepower, they jammed the signal until they could gather enough ground forces to take them out."

"Sounds reasonable," Mueller said. "But why not just bomb the crap out of them? I imagine the PLA wanted prisoners—specific prisoners for interrogation."

Laney's eyebrows rose. "Because they were working with the military?"

"Exactly!"

Laney reached out and placed her hand on her father's arm. "It's a miracle any of us survived this long."

Mueller hung his head. "Many good people didn't make it back."

"Amos, Nesbitt, and the others fought hard, Dad."

"They did and took out a lot of the enemy. If it wasn't for them, none of us would have made it out. Keith took a bullet, and Serenity..." Mueller's voice broke for a moment. "As I ran to get Keith out of the abandoned house, Amos held on to Serenity to keep her from trying to save him—if he hadn't, she would have been blown up. Unfortunately, they came under heavy gunfire, and Amos went down. She took shrapnel."

Ayden imagined the scene—chaotic and deadly like the one at Camp Evergreen.

"Given the destruction of most of the bridges over the Monongahela River, do you believe the military can effectively contain the PLA forces on the opposing side?"

Mueller's mouth twisted. "Not without significant forces to help hold the remaining ones. They need air support. From what Steve has heard so far, our air force is busy out west."

"Do you think it's wise for us to be still monitoring the ham? Although Steve stopped transmitting after we warned him about the compound being a PLA target, how can we be certain it's safe to receive?"

"That's a Steve question, sweetheart. I defer to his expertise in communication matters. But I feel better knowing what's going on in the world."

"Speaking of the world, where are our allies? What are they

doing? What about NATO?" Laney asked, peppering him with the same questions Ayden was wondering.

Mueller took a long sip of his water before answering.

Ayden was on the edge of his seat.

"Here's what we know about that. Britain and Europe were also struck with EMPs and cyberattacks that crippled them as well. Russia or China attacked all our allies located anywhere near them, including Japan, South Korea. We know Australia is fighting alongside US warships off the coast of Florida down through the Caribbean and Puerto Rico. The Gulf of Mexico is secure at the moment, preventing China from reaching the center of the country, which seemed to be their original plan."

Ayden stood and walked around his sister's bed to approach Mueller's. "Do you have any idea how many of China's forces have successfully landed on our shores?"

"As far as we've heard, the People's Liberation Navy (PLAN) has at least twenty ships and accompanying fleet oilers off the East Coast. A Russian-Chinese flotilla was sighted in the Bering Sea the week before the EMP attack. A flotilla of PLAN ships traveled from the Philippine Sea to Vladivostok, Russia, where it was joined by Russian naval ships."

"And our government didn't find that alarming?" Ayden asked.

Mueller winced as he sat up straighter and leaned forward while Laney fluffed his pillows. "They sent some of our naval ships to monitor them after the ten-ship Russian-Chinese flotilla was sighted in the Bering Sea. US forces were monitoring their movement, but Beijing claimed it was a joint maritime patrol of the Northern Sea Route, one of two major shipping lanes across the Arctic, and our military believed them."

Ayden ran his hand over the back of his neck. "And we bought that lie? How did our intelligence community miss this?"

"I have no idea. The day before the EMP attack, two Chinese aircraft carriers equipped with J-15 fighters armed with air-to-air missiles left Jiangnan Shipyard in Shanghai, China. We've heard chatter that between five to ten of PLAN's amphibious warships are headed this way now. Each one is capable of carrying between nine hundred and twelve hundred troops and their associated complement of amphibious assault vehicles, hovercraft, and helicopters."

"And you learned all this from ham radio transmissions?" Ayden asked.

Mueller nodded. "From all over the world—that and lots of conspiracy theories from around the globe suggesting direct US government involvement in the attacks. Not sure I believe any of that."

Ayden told him about witnessing the bombing of the presidential motorcade in Maryland.

"It could have been the designated successor and not the president."

"Like the designated survivor TV show?" Laney asked.

"Yes, sort of. That person is in the presidential line of succession. They're kept in a separate location from that of the president, the vice president, and others in the presidential line of succession to safeguard continuity in the presidency if all the others die."

Ayden pondered that for a moment. It made sense. "Does that mean we now have no one who can step in to be president?"

"No. The surviving official highest in the line of succession would become the acting president."

Laney lowered herself back into her chair. "So if the president, vice president, and other secretaries are all dead, could the Secretary of Homeland Security take the oath?"

Mueller nodded.

"Um…" Laney said. "I seem to recall you saying he was a buffoon or something like that?"

"Among other derogatory names," Monica said, entering the room. She walked over and bent to kiss Mueller on the lips. "Aren't you supposed to be resting?" she asked as she rubbed

Laney's shoulders. "Maybe you can help me while your dad takes a nap."

Laney stood. "Dad never sleeps, but I'd be glad to give you a hand, Mom."

Ayden glanced back at Clara. Drool slid from her mouth. It appeared she'd be out for a while.

"I'd like to help wherever you need me, too."

Monica smiled. "Awesome. We need people in the kitchen and laundry areas." She took Mueller's hand. "With Amos, Nesbitt, and the others gone and needing to increase our patrols, we've had to shift those folks to sentry duties outside the walls."

"Who made that decision?" Mueller asked.

Ayden detected tension regarding that topic.

"The council. They didn't want to bug you with the details while you're healing."

Mueller threw back the covers and dangled one leg over the side of his hospital bed. "I'm fine. I don't know why Doc has me hooked up to this crap." He pulled off the monitor electrodes one by one.

"Stop that!" Monica grabbed him by the shoulder. "You get yourself back in that bed and stay there until Doc clears you." She wagged her finger in his face. "I almost lost you out there, dammit!"

Mueller blinked rapidly as she spoke.

"You're going to follow the doctor's orders and not go running around ripping out stitches and setting your recovery back."

"Yes, ma'am." Mueller pulled his leg back onto the mattress with a scowl.

"If you're good, Daddy"—Laney giggled—"when I return later today, I'll bring you some of Mary's shoofly pie."

A huge smile spread across Mueller's face. "Promise?"

"Only if the doc says you've stayed in bed," Monica said.

Ayden followed Laney and Monica past the surgical bay, where the doctor was working to save Keith. "What is shoofly pie?"

"You've never had it before?" Laney asked. "Oh, you are in for a treat! It is a Pennsylvania Dutch recipe with a super rich filling made of molasses and brown sugar. It's so yummy!"

The surgery suite door opened, and the nurse stepped back, offering Ayden a view of the room. "I'll take a piece when you return," the doctor called as he stood over Keith with a scalpel in his hand.

Laney smiled. "You got it, Doc."

The door of the shipping container turned medical suite creaked as Ayden, Laney, and Monica exited. As he stepped out, Ayden's eyes adjusted to the late morning sun.

"How short are we on security forces?" Laney asked.

Monica held out her hand, directing Ayden toward the shed-like building, where he was told the compound's council members met to discuss the important matters facing the group. "We've doubled the patrols and tightened security checks. We need as much advance notice of any trouble as possible."

"What about Serenity's people in Bowers Township? Can't they alert us as well?"

"They're in disarray with Hugh gone. Serenity's group is closest to us, but they lost one guy, and with Keith in surgery and Serenity badly injured, they're just trying to feed themselves and survive. They're not even doing patrols."

"How's Serenity?" Ayden asked. "I know she left against the doctor's orders." In fact, she'd pulled the IV needle from her hand, got dressed, and demanded to be taken home when she heard that Walt Cayman, her old rival, had escaped from custody. She foolishly thought she could somehow better protect her group by putting her health at risk.

"Sadie visited Keith yesterday," Monica explained. "She took some of Doc's herbal sedatives home to slip into Serenity's tea to make her rest."

"His recipe works," Ayden said. "I slept for several hours after the nurse put some into my tea."

Monica smiled. "It's a good thing they work. Otherwise, Serenity would be trying to climb on a horse to search for Cayman."

"She's that concerned about what he might do to her group?" Laney asked.

"Well, he held her captive at his compound. He and his brother terrorized Bowers Township until they finally fought back. She has cause to feel that way."

"But his followers have been defeated, right? That's what Dad told us."

"As far as we know."

"Should we be concerned about his guy?" Ayden asked.

"He won't come back here. He preys on the weak. We aren't weak."

Ayden nodded, hoping that was the case.

"What about the mansion and Serenity's group?" Laney stopped walking and turned to Monica with a concerned expression. "They're basically defenseless now."

Monica shrugged. "They've set up a few passive defenses around their place. They'll just have to do what they can to defend themselves while Keith and Serenity heal."

"That sucks," Laney said.

As they continued to walk, Ayden thought of Mia and her family in Wyoming, their thousand-acre ranch, and their broader community of fellow ranchers. They were tough folks. He comforted himself with knowing they'd pull together. They weren't defenseless like the people of Bowers Township.

TWO

Mia Christiansen

Christiansen Ranch
Farson, Wyoming
Day Twenty-Two

Four days had passed since the American fighter jets had flown over the Christiansen ranch and annihilated the Russian convoy racing toward them. Since then, the ranch had been hosting a small team of US forces from the Sagebrush Prairie Wind Farm near Lander, Wyoming. Although the ranch remained on high alert, the presence of this team and their ability to communicate with the US forces involved in repelling the invaders provided Mia with a small measure of comfort.

After their arrival, the cowboys had returned to their duties, preparing the ranch's livestock for the long, frigid winter ahead, while Mia Christiansen's father and ranch manager, Dirk, had traveled back and forth for days, making the one-hundred-mile round trip to stock the cabin's firewood supplied from the mountain's fallen trees. Mia's sons—nine-year-old Carter, seven-year-old Luke, and four-year-old Xavier—had been helping them unload the wood and stack it near the cabin's covered back porch. She worried it wouldn't be enough. The roads would become impassable once snow began to fall, and there were no trees in the high desert to cut to keep them warm. Winter was going to be harsh.

Mia set five extra breakfast plates on the dining room table, preparing to share a meal with their guests from the wind farm in Lander. The special forces soldiers had shown up shortly before the US fighter jets blew up the Russian military convoy racing up the highway toward the ranch and beyond it, Iron Mountain and the communication towers.

Across the room, Mia's mother, Melody, removed the biscuits from the dutch oven baking in the living room's oversized fireplace and placed them on a plate. "Luke, run down to the bunkhouse and tell the soldiers breakfast is ready."

"What can I do, Grammy?" Xavier asked, standing at the head of the table.

"You could get the butter from the kitchen counter." Melody tousled his light brown hair.

Xavier's smile widened. "Yes, ma'am!" He turned and ran through the doorway toward the kitchen.

"I hope Dad, Dirk, and Carter make it back before the gravy gets too cold," Mia said as she placed a fork at each place setting.

They'd set out at sunrise in her grandfather's ancient truck with a three-hundred-gallon tank in the bed to collect water from Big Sandy River. Before the lights went out, the ranch had pumped water from a large reservoir to different locations on the pasture or used a semi with a flatbed that carried multiple three-thousand-gallon holding tanks to haul water from area to area. Now, they had to haul water several times a day. She wasn't sure how they'd manage it once the snow began to fall and the water froze. Life was about to become brutal and possibly deadly in Wyoming without electricity or diesel for their generators.

"We'll save enough for them and keep it warm by the fire,"

Melody said. Her mother stopped beside her and leaned close. "Deminski is kinda hot, isn't he?"

Mia smirked. "If you say so."

"You don't think so?"

"I haven't had time to notice."

"Don't get me wrong," Melody continued as she headed toward the door, "the other three are attractive, but Knebel and Osgood are a little rough around the edges." She stopped and touched her finger to her chin. "And I haven't figured Hoehn out yet. He's... well... too quiet."

"They won't be here long enough for you to have to worry about figuring them out, Mom."

"They could. It could start snowing any day. Remember back in 2008 when Lander got nearly thirty inches of snow in two days?"

Mia had been in her teens back then and visiting a girlfriend in Lander. Her father had driven in the snowstorm to get her. They'd spent the night in the truck because the snow was coming down so hard he couldn't see to drive. Her mother had been crazy with worry.

"We don't get as much snow these days," Mia responded.

"I'm just saying—they could be around a while longer. Wouldn't hurt to get to know them, at least Deminski."

"Don't play matchmaker, Mom."

Mia and her mother hadn't spoken much about Ayden since she'd been home, but he was constantly on Mia's mind. She was sick with worry about him and his safety. The last thing on her mind was flirting with the soldiers, who would be leaving anytime now.

"I'm not. I'm just saying."

"Ayden could still come back, you know," Mia said, more to herself than to her mother.

Melody stopped and turned. Mia glanced up. Her mother's expression was filled with sympathy. "I'm so sorry, Mia." Melody rushed to her side and threw her arms around Mia. "I know you must miss him terribly."

Mia burst into tears, finally letting out all the pain and sorrow of missing him. "It's unbearable to think I may never see him again."

Melody leaned back and looked her in the eyes. "I know this. That boy worships you. I could see it in his eyes every time he looked at you—and he adores those boys. He will move heaven and earth to get back here. Don't count him out just yet."

Mia forced a smile and nodded. "I know. I know." She loved that her parents and her boys all loved Ayden.

"You know what?" her father, Neil, asked, entering the room.

"She knows Ayden is on his way here right this minute."

"Of course he is. No doubt about it." Her father pulled out the chair at the head of the table. "You never questioned that, did you?"

Mia said nothing. In fact, she'd questioned everything about it. "Wyoming is a long way to travel from New York without transportation."

"Ayden will figure something out," Carter said, appearing in the doorway.

Mia pulled a chair out for him next to his grandfather.

"Who's in New York?"

Mia glanced back as the soldiers from the wind farm piled into the room.

"You got family in New York?" First Sergeant Shane Deminski rounded the table and stopped at the chair across from Mia.

"Mom's boyfriend is there." Carter poured gravy over his biscuits.

"Oh yeah? What part?"

"Manhattan," Mia said, sadness lacing her tone.

Deminski shared a look with his communications specialist, Terrance Hoehn.

"Do you know anything about what happened there?" Melody asked as she handed Deminski the plate of biscuits.

"Um…" Once again, his gaze shifted to Hoehn.

Hoehn scooted his chair closer to the table, took the napkin, and placed it on his lap before speaking. "As you know, Manhattan is heavily populated. Chaos struck the city almost immediately. Fires raged. Violence broke out." He looked up from his plate as Luke and Xavier took their seats. "But reports are that thousands of people got off the island, flooding into Brooklyn and other boroughs. Most crossed into New Jersey."

"That's what Ayden would have done," Neil said. "He would have headed for New Jersey. He's probably somewhere in Ohio or Indiana, as we speak."

"Could be—if he left right away," Hoehn added.

Mia didn't like the way he'd said it—as if implying Ayden wouldn't have made it off Manhattan if he hadn't left right away.

"What about all those Chinese troops on the East Coast, including Maryland, Pennsylvania, and even into West Virginia and Kentucky?"

"It's just their special forces so far—attempting to secure major routes and critical infrastructure like bridges and rail lines in advance of ground forces," Hoehn said.

"Special forces like the ones you guys encountered at the wind farm?" Neil interjected.

"Those were Russian—the Spetsnaz. Russia's covert Spetsnaz forces are usually assigned these sorts of stealthy, high-risk missions, including an apparent order to capture the bunker. Someone inside the bunker must have alerted the commando unit when we breached the door and took control."

"Must have," Hoehn said. "Because they were hovering over the meadow near the Iron Mountain towers and dropping from helicopters within twelve hours."

"You were there?" Mia asked, leaning in. "It was you on the mountain when they landed."

Deminski glanced around the table at his team. "Yeah. Our primary objective was to seize control of communications at the towers and repair any damage done to the equipment to establish a secure line with our military forces. We need the radio equipment there to gather intelligence about enemy activity, coordinate defenses, and possibly request reinforcements."

Sergeant Rodney Osgood, who was seated to the right of Hoehn, spoke up, "As we approached the towers, the whomp, whomp, whomp of a helicopter echoed through the mountains. At first, some of us thought it could be one of the helo squadrons out of Cheyenne."

"That was me." Hoehn took a sip of water. He put down his glass and continued. "Turned out to be our worst nightmare, I'm afraid. Seconds later, the western sky revealed two gray-green helicopters with red star insignias."

"Shocked the sh—life out of me," Osgood said, glancing at Mia's sons.

Weapons Sergeant Jay Knebel put down his fork. "Not me. I expected trouble. That FBI chick warned us they might want control of the comms towers."

Hoehn nodded.

"I didn't trust her. Thought she might be a traitor, like Gadwell," Osgood murmured.

"Who is he?" Melody asked, handing Osgood the plate of steaks.

Osgood used his fork to place a breakfast steak on his plate. "Some elite with connection to the Chinese."

Knebel forked a steak onto his plate. "Anyway, when Deminski gave the command to engage the Spetsnaz, the team dismounted the ATVs and took off running toward the meadow, and we engaged the Russian soldiers as they emerged from the helicopters."

Mia glanced over at Xavier, concerned the talk of war might frighten him. He was pushing his eggs around his plate and humming, oblivious to the conversation, but Carter and Luke appeared glued to every word. "Boys, why don't you take your plates and eat in the kitchen?"

"Aw, Mom. I want to hear what happened."

"Do what your momma says, boys," her father urged.

Grumbling, the boys gathered their food, but as they walked past her father, he winked. "Don't worry. Pops will tell you all about it later."

"The PG version." Melody gave her husband a stern look.

"Of course." Neil chuckled.

Once the boys were out of earshot, the conversation continued.

"I heard a massive explosion," Mia said, recalling the firefight on the mountain where Reid and the hunter had been gunned down.

"Winters—he was our explosive expert. He fired mortars and struck the two helos. As the shell hit the first one, it burst into flames and crashed into the meadow, taking several Russian soldiers with it," Osgood said.

Mia noticed he was referring to the soldier in the past tense. The fact Winters wasn't with the team indicated he might not have made it off the mountain alive, but she didn't want to ask to confirm it.

Deminski leaned back in his chair and stared out the window behind Mia. "The second helicopter took off, maneuvering to avoid the team's fire. It swerved and disappeared over the ridge out of range of the mortars. The remaining Russian soldiers, now on the ground, opened fire. The firefight was fierce, with both sides taking casualties. Soon after, Winters and Ross fell, taken down by enemy fire raining down from the helicopter." He paused, shifting in his chair and rubbing the back of his neck. "A bullet struck Dixon, one of the wind farm's security guards. I dragged him to cover while Osgood and Knebel continued to pick off the remaining Russians one by one. The fight seemed never-ending, but finally, as the last of the Russian soldiers fell, I ordered my

troops to advance and secure the area around the radio towers."
Deminski looked over at Hoehn, and he continued with the story.

Hoehn glanced around the table. "I immediately worked to
establish communications with the US forces."

"That's when we learned Chinese ground forces are now on the
East Coast and advancing west at pace," Knebel said, shoving a
bite of steak in his mouth as if the whole thing were nothing to be
concerned about.

Mia's stomach tightened. She feared she might be sick. Ayden
didn't stand a chance with ground forces in his path.

"The higher-ups ordered us to maintain control over the radio
towers and the bunker and wait for reinforcements," Osgood said.

"So what are you doing here?" Mia asked through the knot in
her throat.

"Our reinforcements arrived just before that Russian convoy.
They sent us to monitor and report its position," Deminski said.

"You called in the fighter jets?" Neil asked.

"Yep!" Osgood said through a mouth full of biscuits.

"What now?" Mia asked. "What's your mission now?"

"Work with the resistance." Deminski placed his napkin on his
plate and stood. "You guys are the first of the resistance here in
southern Wyoming."

"Us?" Melody said, pushing her chair back and rising to her
feet.

"Yes, you. We need your connections. The folks you organized
to defend your area. We need all of you for the resistance."

"What happened to the reinforcements?" Mia asked.

Deminski stopped in the dining room doorway and glanced
back over his shoulder. "They're guarding Warren Air Force
Base."

THREE

Ayden

___

New Eden Compound
Somerset Township
Washington County, Pennsylvania
Day Twenty-Two

The compound was abuzz with activity as Ayden and Laney followed her mother, Monica, away from the medical building. Some residents were chopping wood, while others hung wet laundry on ropes strung between trees. Even small children had tasks, carrying sticks of wood to a pavilion-like structure where the compound's food was prepared each day.

"I'm going to ride over and visit with Hugh Meecham's family later today," Monica said. She stopped walking. "Don't tell your dad, Laney. He'd have a conniption fit if he knew. But we need to make sure we're all united—in case we need to fight the PLA together. On my way, I'm going to stop in and see Jane Rostrum. She knows Hugh's family well, so I'm hoping to get her to come along to speak with them."

"I could go with you," Laney said. She glanced up at Ayden. "Ayden and I could ride with you."

Ayden shifted his gaze from her to the medical facility.

"Clara's in good hands." Laney's expression grew serious. "It's up to us to ensure this region remains secure so she stays that way."

Ayden scanned the interior of the compound again. As well prepared as they were to defend themselves, they were no match for China's army. He knew they needed every ally they could get just to stay alive. "Sure. Why not? I'll ride with you."

"Maybe we can stop in and check on Serenity on our way back," Laney suggested.

Monica smiled. "You like that kid, don't you?"

"She's got grit, as Grandpa used to say," Laney said. "I admire that. She's no victim."

Monica nodded. "She was homeless, living on the streets before the lights went out. That'll make you tough."

"Or hardened. Maybe a little stubborn." Ayden had seen that in her when she left against her mother and the doctor's wishes. And just the day before, when she returned to check on her father, who was doing better at the time. She and Mueller were discussing what had gone wrong in Clairton before the PLA attacked them and blew up her father and Mueller with a mortar. Serenity was insisting Mueller order his crew to go out and search for someone —now he knew that someone was Walt Cayman. When Mueller told her to forget about him, that he was no threat to anyone, she'd pounded her hand on Mueller's bed, yelling she'd go after him herself. She wasn't thinking straight. The doctor said it was due to the emotional and physical trauma. Ayden could see that. He and Clara had experienced enough of both. At times, he had made poor choices, and he was a grown man, not a sixteen-year-old girl.

"Join me at the command center." Monica suggested. "Given your firsthand experience with PLA attacks, both of you might have valuable input to share."

Ayden closed his eyes for a second to savor the breeze blowing through a tiny window in New Eden's governing council meeting space. Monica and Laney had led him there to discuss their plan to visit Hugh Meecham's family later that day. Ayden took a seat in the corner of the shed turned command post. He was impressed. Shelves full of books, including Robert's Rules of Order, lined its walls. One prominently displayed a bound copy of the United States Constitution. In the center of the room, a large wooden slab sat on top of a few crates. Gathered around it were New Eden's council members.

This was his first proper introduction to the group that held New Eden together. Ayden noted the weary lines etched around each member's eyes and mouths. Before they began, Monica introduced him to the council.

"This is Ayden Miller. He's the one who helped my Laney get home and found Ty and Keith in Clairton." She went around the table. "Jake is a former police officer. He oversees the compound's security."

Jake nodded a greeting.

"To his right is Mariah, a former schoolteacher, and on his left is Peggy. She holds a degree in horticulture and manages our sustainable food production. Across from Jake is Frank Sonderborg, a military veteran and the group's weapons and defensive skills instructor. He's in charge of setting up our defenses and getting everyone ready to face the enemy."

"I hear you've seen them up close and personal, Ayden," Frank said.

"Too close."

"I'd like to debrief you sometime today. Mueller and Lancy both shared their observations of the PLA's weapons and tactics. Now, I'm curious about what you saw in Maryland."

"I'd be glad to tell you everything I know—which isn't much."

"Every bit of intel helps," Frank said.

Ayden nodded. He wasn't sure how, but he was happy to help.

"Steve is our emergency communications director. His role is crucial, especially now that reliable communication with the outside world is so vital."

"Laney and I spoke to Owen Graff about what occurred," Steve said, addressing the council rather than Ayden. "It's something we need to consider. The Chinese still have satellites that can see our towers. I don't know what technology they might possess to indicate who might be able to send and receive radio transmissions. We have to assume the worst."

"I spoke with Ty about that this morning," Monica said. "He wants us to continue listening."

"Even if it means they are able to pinpoint our location?" Peggy asked.

Monica didn't respond.

"I say we vote on it," Mariah said.

"Yes!" Peggy agreed. "I move to cease receiving or transmitting ham transmissions and"— she paused and glanced over at Steve—"and take down the towers so the enemy satellites can't spot them."

"Wait!" Frank urged.

"I second the motion," Mariah said.

"All in favor," Peggy said.

"You can't do that. You aren't the chairperson," Monica argued.

"I'm the chairperson pro tem. He's not here. That makes me the acting chair." Peggy stood with her hands on the table. "All in favor, say aye!"

Everyone but Monica and Frank said yes.

"The ayes have it. Steve, let us know how we can help you take down the towers," Peggy said.

Steve rubbed his temples. "I'll get on it right after the meeting."

As the meeting continued, Ayden hung on every detail. Frank and Jake took turns outlining the status of their defenses, with Jake reporting on the latest patrol findings.

Monica cleared her throat. "That brings me to why I asked Laney and Ayden to join us. I'd like to take them along to visit Hugh Meecham's family to see if we can gain their cooperation with our defense. I know Ty and Meecham met and reached an agreement, but after what happened in Clairton, I want to make sure they're still on board. We really need them to take charge of all of Bowers Township and get those folks involved."

Ayden recalled Serenity and her mother, Sadie, talking about how the PLA had killed Hugh and his son, Cody, on that mission to Clairton. Their family was still in the throes of grief and had lost their leader. He imagined it would be tough for them to rebound and continue the fight.

Jake leaned forward, his fingers interlaced on the table. "What does Ty think of this plan?"

"He doesn't know, and you aren't going to tell him. He nearly died on that mission. Now, he needs to recover."

"Um…Ty's going to blow his top if we keep that from him," Frank said.

Monica's gaze bored into him. "You let me worry about my husband."

"It sounds like you're not asking for our permission, so what are you after?" Jake queried.

"Something to offer them."

"Offer them? Why?"

"I don't know. When Tyson met with them, he brought weapons and ammunition." She frowned. "And that awful Walt Cayman."

"What happened to him afterward?" Frank asked.

Monica shrugged. "Tyson said he handed him over and there would be a trial of some kind. Ty and the others left soon after. Somehow, Cayman escaped."

"Yeah? We need to inform our security teams. I don't trust him not to come back here," Frank said.

"What can he do? His guys are gone."

"Can't say, but I wouldn't put it past him to join the PLA just to get even with us."

"Maybe you should come along, Frank," Laney said. "If this Walt character is so dangerous, you should find out what's happened to him. Help them find the guy."

Ayden was amazed at how complicated life had become. Along with struggling to feed themselves, they had to take on the role of the police, justice system, and military—the authorities that had once held society together.

"I have drills the rest of this morning, but I can meet back here at thirteen hundred hours to head over to Bowers Township," Frank said.

"I plan to stop in to see Jane Rostrum on the way. She's a calming presence. I think she'd be a valuable asset in getting this off the ground," Monica said.

When the meeting adjourned, Ayden approached Frank. "I'd like to learn more about the drills you're teaching—weapons and self-defense."

Frank's assessing look made Ayden brace himself, but then the veteran nodded and raised an eyebrow. "You want me to teach you how to handle a rifle and hand-to-hand combat?" He snickered. "From the look of your battered face, son…you need it."

Ayden touched his cheek and ran a finger over the gash above his right eye. They were just a few of the injuries he'd sustained from fighting since the lights went out. "I do." He chuckled.

"I'd be glad to teach you. You can start now if you want."

"How about tomorrow? I need to make sure my sister is settled in before I leave on our trip to Bowers Township."

"Very well," Frank said. "We start at zero five hundred hours."

"What time is that?"

"Five o'clock in the morning."

Ayden grimaced. "That early?"

"The enemy doesn't wait for the sun to come up to attack."

Ayden recalled being jolted awake when the PLA attacked Camp Evergreen.

"I guess not. I'll be there." He swallowed hard. "At zero five hundred hours."

FOUR

Ayden

Rocky Top Equestrian Center
Washington County, Pennsylvania
Day Twenty-Two

It was fairly late in the day by the time Ayden, Laney, Monica, and Frank piled into the compound's vintage Ford F350 Crew Cab pickup and headed north to Bowers Township. To reach it, they had to pass through two checkpoints guarded by Bowers Township residents. The ragtag sentries appeared jumpy as Frank explained who they were and why they were there. At the first roadblock, they were forced to wait for nearly an hour while a rider rode his bicycle to Jane Rostrum's to seek permission for them to visit her.

Rolling green hills dotted with trees stretched for miles, their leafy canopies waving gently in the soft afternoon breeze. The undulating landscape was broken here and there by smaller family-owned farms, whose red barns and white farmhouses added splashes of color. After crossing a set of railroad tracks that acted as the eastern boundary, Ayden got his first glimpse of the Rostrums' horse ranch with its round pens for exercising horses and the shiny roofs of the stables. To the left of the tracks, a white-clad farmhouse sat on a hill overlooking a vast pasture. The gravel drive curved to the right, and they encountered a gate. Above it, a sign indicated they'd reached Rocky Top Equestrian Center. To his right, a teenage boy rushed from one of the barns to open the gate. He waved the pickup through and then shut it behind them. A woman in her early sixties stood in the doorway of the first horse barn. Frank stopped the vehicle near the opening.

"Jane," Monica said. "It's been ages."

A young, sandy-haired boy stepped out from behind Jane. He waved to them as he crossed in front of the vehicle and headed toward the round pen, where two horses stood with their necks extended over the white fence surrounding the pen.

"Finn has gotten so big!" Monica said, exiting the Ford.

"He'll be seven in October," Jane said.

As Ayden and the others exited the vehicle, Monica approached Jane, and the two women hugged.

"Where has the time gone?" Monica asked.

"It flew by," Jane replied. "Serenity told me your daughter made it home."

Monica glanced back at Laney, who was exiting the truck.

"She did. We're so grateful to Ayden here…" She held her hand out to him, and he rushed over and took it. "He ran into her at Harpers Ferry, West Virginia, and helped her reach us."

Jane smiled. She moved toward Ayden with her arms outstretched. "I hear we have you to thank for finding Serenity and Keith as well." After a brief hug, Ayden stepped back, uncomfortable with the attention. He understood their gratitude at their loved ones' return, but he'd only been in the right place at the right time. He hadn't done anything more than give them a ride.

"How are Serenity and Keith?" Jane asked.

"Serenity made it through her surgery fine. Doc says she just needs time to heal now. Keith was having his second surgery when we left. He survived the first, but Doc had to stop when his blood pressure kept dropping. He waited as long as he could before he went back in to find the last of the bleeding. Doc said Keith's chances of survival were about twenty percent."

"They'd be zero if Ayden hadn't found him," a man said, stepping out from the shadow of the barn. He approached and extended a gloved hand. "Doctor McCluskey. I was planning to take a ride over to see if Doctor Hendricks needed a hand, but it seems he has everything under control, given the circumstances. I'm not sure what more I could offer his patients."

"How's Tyson?" Jane asked.

"Sore and stubborn. He took a bullet to his arm and was nearly blown up, but he claims he's fine and wants to get back to running the compound," Monica said.

"Sounds like him." Jane smiled.

Monica stepped back and gestured to where Frank was leaning against the vehicle. "Do you know Frank? He's on the security team of our community."

"I don't believe we've met." Jane nodded a greeting.

"Lovely place you have here," Frank said.

"It was." Jane's voice held a hint of sadness. "Before the addition of sandbag fortifications and foxholes."

"Sign of the times," Frank muttered.

"I hear you have some pretty impressive walls around your place," Jane said.

"Ty and the group started them a while before the lights went out. The neighbors up the road reported us to the township, the county, the state, and the feds, trying to stop us."

Frank nodded. "If we hadn't had so many hoops to jump through and cease and desist orders put against us, we would have almost finished by the time the dung hit the fan."

"I'm so sorry about Hugh and his son," Monica said.

Jane thanked her. "His family is devastated. It's a huge blow to the whole community. Hugh was our de facto leader. The void is massive. Everyone is in shock and unsure of what to do next."

"That's understandable," Monica said. "I met Hugh the day before they set out for Clairton on the supply run. He seemed like an excellent leader. Tyson respected him enough to seek him out for joint cooperation between our two communities."

"What I want to know is how we protect ourselves from the People's Liberation Army forces," Dr. McCluskey said.

"So far, the US forces have held them at bay on the opposite side of the Monongahela River," Laney said.

"How long can that last?" Dr. McCluskey asked. "I heard they were only the advance teams, and the rest of their ground forces haven't even landed yet."

"Unfortunately, that's what we've heard as well," Frank said.

"In light of this new information—the PLA are the more deadly enemy. Do you guys have a new plan?"

"That's why we're here. We wanted to confirm your community is still on board with the plan to work together for the defense of the region."

Jane glanced over at Dr. McCluskey. "I haven't spoken to the Meechams about that specifically. I received a visit from Wendall Hepworth, the chairman of Bowers Township's Board of Supervisors. With the void of leadership, he thinks he's going to step in and take charge. He actually came here this morning to make sure we were still going to provide the subdivisions with meat, milk, and produce."

"He sounds like a piece of work," Monica said.

"Why don't you folks come up to the house? I can explain just how bad he is." Jane stepped onto the gravel driveway near the vehicle and turned toward her house. "And we can talk about Walt Cayman and our other concerns."

FIVE

Serenity Jones

Byers Mansion
Bowers Township
Washington County, Pennsylvania
Day Twenty-Two

The door to Serenity Jones's Byers Mansion bedroom squeaked open, and a shadowy face appeared in the opening. Her first thought was of Walt Cayman, the man who had terrorized her ever since the lights went out. She froze for a moment, somewhere between terror and rage.

"Are you awake, Serenity?" Jacob, her thirteen-year-old brother, asked.

Tension leaked from her body. "I am now."

The stitches that closed the wound in Serenity's abdomen pulled as she eased over onto her side to face the door. Five days earlier, she'd been hit by shrapnel in a PLA attack in Clairton. She'd watched her close friend, Cody Meecham, die on the floor of an abandoned warehouse during the attack. They'd lost his father,

Hugh—a man Serenity thought of as a mentor—and Joe, her father's friend.

Her father, Keith, had been shot and then had a house blown up around him. He'd miraculously survived and was recuperating in the medical clinic at New Eden, Mueller's fortified compound. Their plan to acquire supplies to build up their defenses around the mansion was thwarted. And now, they and the residents of Bowers Township were helpless against a PLA attack.

"I'm sorry to wake you, sis. But I wanted to tell you your dad is back in surgery. A sentry from New Eden stopped by to let us know."

Serenity tried to sit up.

"Don't!" Jacob ran over to her. "Mom will get mad at me for disturbing you."

"My dad's back in surgery, and they weren't going to tell me?" Serenity asked through gritted teeth.

"He's finally strong enough for the doctor to go back in and close up his wounds. Liz told me it was just routine. Nothing to be concerned about."

"Now your stepmother thinks she's a doctor?"

"No, but…"

"But?"

"I don't know. It's just what she said. I knew you'd be pissed if I didn't tell you."

"You're a good brother, Jacob."

"That's not what you were saying yesterday when I was helping you up the stairs."

"I told you I wanted to stay downstairs in the library."

"Mom said no. She said you wouldn't rest there."

"Whose side are you on, little brother?"

The room filled with candlelight as her mother, Sadie, stepped inside, glaring at Jacob. "The side of getting you better."

"Aren't you supposed to be helping Cheryl and Staci at the gate, son?"

"Yes, ma'am." Jacob turned toward the door. Before exiting, he stopped and looked back at them. "We're having deer stew for dinner. One got caught in the booby traps you and—" He sucked in a quick breath and went silent.

Cody! Her mind finished for him.

Serenity looked away, grief gripping her heart. She and Cody had been growing close. Two days before he died, he'd helped her install booby traps in the densely forested, wild tangle of undergrowth and thick understory surrounding Byers Mansion's twenty-acre property. Together with the group her father had met at the pizzeria in Whitaker, Pennsylvania, they set up pits and laid some sharp defenses in the woods using rusty tools, broken metal pieces, and anything they could to make sharp spikes.

They'd strung old metal fencing and barbed wire to slow intruders down, along with boards with nails sticking out of them, and placed broken pieces of glass into pit traps. She'd fretted more about an attack by Walt Cayman than by an advanced military. Serenity now felt naive to have thought those things might protect them from an advancing army with drones and armored vehicles.

Jacob's stepmother, Liz, entered Serenity's room with his sleeping baby brother wrapped in a shawl against her chest. She held a cup of tea. "It's time for your pain meds, Serenity," she said, stepping around Sadie and placing the cup on the nightstand next to the bed. She grabbed the pill bottle next to the oil lamp and uncapped it. "You don't want to get behind on these. It'll be hard to control the pain if you miss a dose."

"I'm okay. Save them for Dad. He'll need them when he comes home."

"You think you don't need them because you haven't gone without them yet. Trust me, Renny. You don't want to go through that when you don't have to."

Serenity shook her head. A wave of nausea overtook her. "I don't want them. They make my head too fuzzy."

Sadie opened her mouth to protest, but Liz cut her off.

"Okay, sweetheart." Liz smirked. "Just drink the tea. You need to keep hydrated."

Sadie had suppressed a smile and helped Serenity to a seated position.

"I better get back to the gate," Jacob said. "I'll bring you some stew later."

"No, I'll come down to eat. I need to get up and walk. I can't lie here and do nothing."

"Sure, baby girl. Right after you drink your tea." Sadie held the cup out to Serenity.

SIX

Ayden

Rocky Top Equestrian Center
Washington County, Pennsylvania
Day Twenty-Two

Jane led them up the driveway to a two-story farmhouse with a columned, wraparound stone porch. Its white-washed swing swayed in the breeze. A bed of red roses stretched along the front of the house. Nearby stood a tall, grand oak tree supporting an old tire swing. As they neared the detached garage near the house, Ayden glanced to his right at the twenty-five-foot radio tower. His gut immediately twisted. "You have a ham radio?"

"Had," Jane said. "It's fried."

Ayden turned to Frank. "Could the Chinese have a list of ham operators?"

Frank nodded. "Ham operators have to have a license from the Federal Communications Commission. It's public information, including names and mailing addresses."

"Then they know about that," Ayden said, pointing to the radio tower.

"Yes."

Ayden quickened his steps. "You're not safe here," he told Jane as they approached a side door to her home. She stopped with her hand on the doorknob. Her gaze shifted from Ayden to the tower.

"And where would we go?"

The young boy from the barn rounded the corner of the house from the back lawn, holding on to the collar of a small black-and-tan beagle. "We could go to Byers Mansion. It has plenty of rooms, and the bad guys wouldn't know we were there."

"This is my grandson, Finn," Jane said.

He walked up to Ayden, released his grip on his dog's collar, and extended his hand. "Pleased to make your acquaintance." He gestured to his beagle. "This is Gunner."

Something about the boy reminded Ayden of Luke, Mia's seven-year-old son. He was also very outgoing and polite.

"Pleasure to meet you, Finn. How old are you?"

"Six. I'll be seven on October 13. Grandma Jane was going to take me on a tour of the Center for Nanotechnology for my birthday. It's in Baltimore, but I'm not sure we can go there now. It's probably closed now after the electromagnetic pulse attack. They wouldn't have electricity to run their transmission electron microscope or the atomic force microscopes."

Jane's face beamed as she stared down at him. "Finn is interested in science and technology, particularly nanotechnology."

"I'm an inventor!"

"So you're pretty smart then," Ayden said.

"I was in the second grade and was supposed to advance to the fourth grade in the fall. But I can't go to school now."

"He's very intelligent," Jane said.

"And cute!" Laney smiled at him.

Finn blushed and wrapped his arm around his dog.

Jane stepped back from the door and turned to face Ayden. "How long do we have?"

Monica shot Ayden a look. "I don't think they're tracking down every ham operator, Jane."

Jane pushed open the door and led them through a mudroom into the kitchen. A man in his sixties, a young mother, and two small children sat at the table.

"Ruben, this is Monica, her daughter, Laney, and their friends, Ayden and Frank," Jane said, introducing them.

The man stood and extended a hand to Ayden. "Ruben Thomas." He gestured to the woman and children. "My daughter-in-law, Brenda, and my grandchildren, Cherry and James."

The woman nodded a greeting and continued feeding her children.

Monica, Laney, Ayden, and Frank followed Jane through the kitchen to the living room, where a built-in bookcase flanked a stone fireplace. The walls were adorned with smiling family photographs, and off the entry was a beveled glass door that led to a cozy mahogany library filled with books.

"Have a seat," Jane said, gesturing to the sofa pressed against a wall opposite a large window that overlooked the front lawn and the stables in the distance. "Can I get anyone a glass of water or perhaps a refreshing mint tea?" she asked.

"I'd love a mint tea," Monica said, smiling.

As Jane returned to the kitchen, Monica admonished Ayden for scaring Jane. "We need her to help us organize this community. Her running off won't help us—or her neighbors."

"But if all the ham operators' information was public, she and her family could be in danger. Better to leave now before the PLA makes it across the river, right?"

Monica glowered at him. "We have three people in critical condition at our place. There are both elderly and children to consider. We can't load up and run. It's crucial for us to have these folks join forces and fight alongside us."

"Shouldn't that be their choice?" Ayden asked.

"Our choice for what?" Finn asked, plopping down in a wing-backed chair. His beagle sat at his feet, staring at Ayden.

No one spoke.

"Is this about Grandpa Jim's radio?" Finn asked.

Monica smiled. "It's nothing to be worried about, Finn. The US military has everything under control."

"We heard bombs exploding all night," Finn said. He reached down and rubbed his dog's head. "Gunner was scared. So were Sofia and Mateo."

"I was not!" a little boy yelled from the stairs.

"You were, too, Mateo!" the older girl beside him snarked.

"Both of you get back upstairs and finish putting away your laundry," a Hispanic woman said, entering the living room from a hallway on Ayden's right. In her arms was an infant aged maybe eight or nine months. "I'm sorry they interrupted your conversation."

"Not at all, Maria," Monica said.

Before she could turn and leave, Frank called her name. "Maria, how is Raul?"

Monica had filled Ayden in somewhat on the attack that had taken the life of Jane's husband and Maria's daughter.

She stepped back into the room. "Okay. Dr. M has done an amazing job for both of us." As she ventured deeper into the living room, Ayden spotted the bandage on her left thigh.

This family had paid a heavy price already. If the PLA came for them, what chance did they have with small children and injured adults to protect?

The door banged open, and a fourteen-year-old Hispanic boy with deep-set eyes and lanky limbs walked inside. "Danny and Tanner are here!"

Jane rushed from the kitchen, and everyone followed her out onto the porch as two young men in their twenties rode a dirt bike up the driveway.

They stopped at the foot of the porch steps. "We've got trouble!" the older of the two said, breathing hard.

"At the checkpoint?" Jane asked, moving down the stairs toward him.

"No!" He swallowed hard. "The PLA got across the river."

"Where?" Frank said, approaching the edge of the porch. "Where are they?"

"They crossed at Brownsville. Right now, they're fighting locals there, but we've heard reports of Chinese fighter jets bombing sites along the turnpike."

"That's too close." Maria limped over. "That's only twenty miles from here."

Ruben placed a hand on her arm. "Our military will stop them."

Ayden glanced up at the ham radio antennae attached to the garage, and a hard knot formed in his stomach. He touched Monica's arm. She jumped as if he'd poked her with a hot iron. "I'm sorry," he said. "But we need to get back and warn the compound."

"What about us?" Maria asked, cradling her infant tighter to her chest.

Finn stepped out from behind her. "We should go to the mansion. They've got a bomb shelter there."

Jane spun around. "There is? How do you know that?"

"Jacob and I found it when I was there the other day."

Monica brushed past Jane. "Load up, Jane. Take your family to the mansion. We have to get home and prepare our community. We'll send you help if we can."

Ayden was following Monica and Laney down the steps when the garage exploded. An enormous fireball filled with debris launched into the air above it. The sound and shock wave resonated through Ayden's body. Beside him, Monica was screaming, but he could barely hear her over the ringing in his ears. Laney grabbed her arm and pulled her to her feet as the house occupants emerged onto the porch.

"Get everyone out of the house. Run!" Monica screamed.

Ayden shot to his feet, grabbed a young girl in his arms, and ran toward the pickup. Beside him, Laney held the hand of Jane's grandson, Finn—his dog running at his side.

Frank raced past them, flung open the driver's side door, and had the vehicle started by the time Ayden reached it.

Ayden yanked open one of the rear doors and tossed the child inside before turning back toward the house.

"Mom!" Laney yelled.

"I'll get her," Ayden said, sprinting toward the porch, dodging burning debris in the driveway.

Before he reached the steps, Monica emerged from the house. Behind her was Maria with her infant. "My husband! My children!" Maria yelled. She spun back around. "I have to get my husband and other children."

"Where's Jane?" Monica asked, grabbing Ayden's arm.

"I don't know," he said, turning back toward the vehicle.

"Grammy Jane!" Finn yelled.

Seconds later, she and the two young men emerged from the barn, leading a string of unsaddled horses.

Ruben appeared at the back of the Ford with his daughter-in-law.

"Cherry! James!" Brenda screamed.

Ruben picked up the little girl from the back of the vehicle and handed her to her mother.

"Where's James!" she cried.

Has the child gotten lost in the confusion? Ayden thought.

"The garage!" Brenda screamed, racing up the drive toward it. Ruben set out after her.

Ayden and Monica passed her as they ran toward the vehicle. Ayden squeezed himself into the back seat just as a second explosion hit the farmhouse.

～

Minutes after a second drone strike leveled her home, Jane Rostrum, along with the only survivors, her grandson, Finn and his beagle, Gunner, and the two Meecham brothers had hitched a horse trailer to the back of Monica's old Ford pickup and stowed themselves inside for the trip to the mansion. Ayden had argued against stopping there first, even though it was on the way. He was anxious to get back to New Eden and keep his sister safe. The fifteen-minute drive to the mansion was pure torture, as his mind imagined a similar strike against New Eden coming at any moment. Clara could barely walk, let alone flee unseen bombs dropping from the sky.

When they pulled up to the gate in front of a one-hundred-year-old mansion, Jane, Finn, and Gunner piled out and hurried up the drive as Danny and Tanner quickly unhitched the horse trailer.

Jacob, Serenity's little brother, was full of questions. "What happened? Where are Raul and the others?"

"Get inside, Jacob," Danny ordered. "Gather everyone in the dining room, and then we'll explain."

Tanner appeared at the driver's door. "Thanks for the lift."

"You should get everyone inside the bunker and stay there," Frank said.

"How long?"

"As long as you can." Frank put the old Ford into gear and sped away.

SEVEN

Serenity

Byers Mansion
Bowers Township
Washington County, Pennsylvania
Day Twenty-Two

Serenity stirred as she heard raised voices downstairs. She strained to hear and could make out that Tanner and his brother, Danny, were among them. She tried to sit up, but her head felt like it weighed a ton. Her brain was still fuzzy from the tea her mother had given her. She gently rolled onto her side and called out, hoping someone would hear her. A moment later, the door opened, and six-year-old Finn McKeowen's face appeared in the opening.

"Hi there, little man. What are you doing here?"

"The Chinese blew up our house, so we had to come here," he said in his usual frank manner.

"Finn!" Jane called from the hall. "Come away and let her sleep!"

"I gotta go!" Finn turned back toward the door.

Serenity pushed back the covers, determined to climb out of

bed and go downstairs to see what was going on. She was just about to inch her legs over the side of the bed when an explosion rattled the house. She rolled out of bed, landing hard on her right shoulder. Pain from the incision in her abdomen caused her to see stars.

Finn rushed to her side. "Are you okay?"

"What was that?"

"It sounded like fireworks on the Fourth of July," Finn said over the sound of Gunner's barking. Finn ran to the window. "I see fire."

"Where?" Serenity asked, managing to get to her knees.

"Outside—by the stables." Finn ran to the door.

Gunner skittered out of the room as Serenity reached for her rifle, leaning against the wall between the bed and the dresser. She had just brought it up to her shoulder when Tanner burst through the door.

"Serenity, you and Finn follow me!" Tanner barked.

Finn ran to Serenity. "Help her."

Tanner rushed across the room and grabbed hold of Serenity's arm, hoisting her to her feet.

Pain shot through her body. She swayed, the blood rushing to her head. "What's going on out there?" she groaned.

Tanner ignored her question. "Can you walk?"

"I think so," she said, placing her rifle's sling over her shoulder.

Finn took her hand, and the two of them led Serenity into the hallway.

Tanner released her and shouldered his weapon before leading them down the hall, and then they crept down the pitch-black back stairs.

Gunfire erupted from the side of the house, and Tanner halted halfway to the bottom. "Back! Get back upstairs!"

Serenity winced, her hand instinctively moving to her abdomen where the shrapnel had torn through. The fresh staples from her recent surgery still tugged painfully at her skin with every movement. Despite the discomfort, she turned and followed Finn back to the landing, Tanner close on their heels.

She stopped by one of the upstairs windows staring out onto the partially lit front lawn. Danny and Jacob were crouched behind sandbags near the walkway leading to the front door. Flames from the barn danced in the shadows on the walls.

Tanner pushed past Serenity and Finn and led them to the grand staircase at the end of the hallway. The nausea and dizziness from the pain and herbal pain reliever caused Serenity to descend the stairs slower than any of them liked. By the time she reached the foyer, her ears were ringing so loud she could barely make out the gunfire outside.

"Is it Walt Cayman?" Serenity asked.

"No! Hurry!" Tanner shouted. "This way!" he said, the light on his scope raking across the floor. "We have to make it to the basement," he yelled, waving them on.

As Tanner threw back the door to the basement, Finn stopped to shout for Gunner, who stood at the front door, barking.

"Go, Finn!" Serenity nudged Finn to go down and turned to watch the front door.

"Gunner, come, boy!" Serenity yelled at the dog.

"Gunner!" Finn called from the bottom of the stairs.

The dog ran past Tanner and Serenity and joined Finn at the bottom of the stairs.

Serenity looked into the dimly lit basement. She could barely make out Finn's features. She looked back, and Tanner was running toward the door.

"Get down there, Serenity. I'm going to help Jacob and my brother," he said before disappearing.

Finn rushed back up the stairs and closed the door behind him. Then he took Serenity's hand. "I've got you!"

She descended the stairs, clutching her rifle to her chest and Finn's hand with the other.

"What's going on, Serenity? What was that noise? Where is everyone?" Leah cried as Serenity and Finn moved deeper into the basement. In her hands, she held a small flashlight pointed into Serenity's eyes.

Serenity reached out and took the light from her hand, pointing it at the floor near Leah's feet. "Shush, Leah. I need to hear."

"Where's my momma?" Leah cried.

"I don't know, sweetie." Serenity scanned the room with the flashlight. "How'd you get down here?"

"Momma and Geneva. They came down with me, and when we heard the loud boom, Momma told me to wait here. They went back upstairs."

Finn pulled another flashlight off a shelf at the bottom of the stairs and flicked it on.

Even with two flashlights illuminating the space, the basement was still a creepy place. Serenity wanted to go upstairs and see what was going on—help defend the mansion—but she was much too weak and dizzy. She wasn't sure she'd even make it up the stairs. She moved to the back corner of the basement and lowered herself onto a stack of boxes.

Leah crawled up beside her, while Finn and Gunner sat on the floor near her feet.

Time passed at a glacial pace as they waited, listening to the muffled sound of gunfire. Then, suddenly, the basement door banged open, and a bloody woman appeared. It wasn't until she said Serenity's name that the teenager realized it was Mallory. Behind her were Jane, Tanner, and Danny. Seconds later, Sadie, Jacob, Geneva, and Liz, holding the baby, streamed inside.

"Where's Staci and Cheryl?" Serenity asked as Tanner slammed the door shut.

"They're gone!" Tanner said, trying to catch his breath.

Danny was putting pressure on a large wound in Mallory's stomach, while Tanner and Jacob shoved a stack of crates aside to reveal a hidden door. Tanner yanked on the latch and pushed open the door before motioning for Danny.

"Lower Mallory down to me, then help Serenity," Tanner called as he jumped down into a tunnel Serenity never knew existed.

"Where does this lead?" she asked.

"The bunker," Finn said.

Danny and Jacob helped Mallory as Serenity and Finn lit the way.

"Take my hand, Serenity," Danny said, standing on the steps down into the tunnel.

"Are you sure it's safe in there?" she asked, inching toward him.

"It's fine, sis. Just hurry, please, before they find us down here," Jacob entreated.

"Who?" Leah asked behind her. "Before who finds us?"

No one answered her.

Danny held Serenity's hand until she reached the last step, then turned to help Leah and the others as Serenity moved toward Tanner and the lamplight at the end of the tunnel. Jacob called for Gunner, and Serenity heard the hatch shut.

She had to fight back a severe case of claustrophobia that threatened to send her into a panic attack. Then she felt her world spin, and a wave of nausea hit her.

Serenity woke up even stiffer and sorer than before. Inhaling deeply, she struggled to understand the unfolding events. The bunker was pitch-black. She heard the noise of several people breathing. Under her right hand, Serenity felt Gunner's soft fur. She reached over and found Leah curled on her side next to her on the makeshift bed. She remembered there had been a gunfight, and they had fled to the bunker.

"What's going on?" she croaked through a dry throat.

"I don't hear them anymore," Finn said.

A battery-operated lantern flicked on and lit up the interior of the World War Two bunker. It was crowded with ten adults, three children, and a beagle dog. The walls were lined with bags and boxes. Jacob was perched on a stack of crates next to the door.

Across from her, Tanner sat on the floor, cleaning his rifle.

"How long do you think we'll have to stay down here?" Serenity asked.

"Probably just until morning. They've likely searched the entire farm and given up on finding us by then," Tanner said.

"They? Who attacked us? What did they want?" Serenity asked.

Tanner hesitated.

"What's going on, Tanner?"

He rose and then took a seat on the crate next to her. "Serenity, the stables and the mansion are gone."

Serenity gasped, and her hand shot up to cover her mouth. Tears stung her eyes, but she held them back.

"The PLA found us," he continued. "Followed us from Jane's."

Serenity shifted her gaze to her friend. Her red-rimmed eyes spoke volumes.

"Raul? Maria and the kids?"

"We were the only survivors," Jane said. Her lips trembled as she stroked one of Gunner's floppy ears.

"What are we going to do now?" Serenity asked, wiping away tears.

Tanner hesitated again.

"We're going to Mexico," Tanner whispered.

"Mexico?"

"Canada isn't an option. Ontario has fallen from what we've heard."

"When are you leaving?"

"Tonight, after we make sure the PLA has left the area. My

family and I are going to load supplies onto the old-school bus and head south."

"But my dad can't travel yet."

There was a long silence before Tanner responded, "I have an obligation to my family—what's left of it."

Serenity swallowed hard. He was going, with or without her father. "I can't go. I can't leave my dad."

"I assumed as much. I wish we could wait, but…"

Serenity thought of Jacob and Sadie. She couldn't decide for them.

"If my mom and brother choose to come with you…" Serenity took a deep breath, fighting back tears. "Will you look after them for me?"

Tanner took her hand in his. "Yes," he whispered.

He moved the battery-powered lantern and set it down beside Mallory. It was the first time Serenity had seen the extent of her injuries. She couldn't believe the woman was still alive after losing so much blood. Tanner felt Mallory's neck for a pulse and then flicked off the light.

"Is she…?" Serenity said, stopping herself from saying it.

Tanner sighed heavily. "Yes."

EIGHT

Ayden

Rocky Top Equestrian Center
Washington County, Pennsylvania
Day Twenty-Two

Each mile was marked with tension as the Ford F350 rolled on toward Laney's community. Ayden's mind whirled with fear as he imagined a drone strike against New Eden coming at any moment. As they neared their destination, about a mile from the compound, the true extent of the devastation began to reveal itself. Just ahead, the remnants of one of New Eden's roadblocks appeared. Debris littered the road, and the haphazard pile of vehicles that once formed a makeshift barricade was disjointed and mangled. Twisted metal and shards of glass were strewn across the area, and some cars were on their side or torn open, revealing their charred interiors. The bodies of fallen sentries lay intermingled with the debris in unnatural positions, some partially under the wreckage of the vehicles, others more visible among the scattered remains.

The air was thick with the acrid smell of burning rubber. Plumes of smoke still rose from smoldering sections of the wreckage, drifting into the sky. The aftermath of the drone strike was a terrible sight to behold.

Monica gasped.

Laney's hand flew up to her mouth as Frank, driving with steely focus, slowed the truck approaching the devastated checkpoint. The tension in the vehicle grew stronger, the air thick with unspoken fear. Monica leaned forward from the passenger seat, peering through the windshield at the chaotic scene that blocked their path.

"What the hell happened here?" she murmured, her voice barely above a whisper.

"Drone strike." Frank brought the truck to a stop a safe distance from the wreckage.

He was the first to move, shoving open the driver's side door. "Stay put. I'm going to look for survivors."

Monica slid over into the driver's seat with caution as he moved through the wreckage. But there was no one left alive. The ferocity of the PLA's attack had robbed them of a chance to make a desperate last stand.

As Frank cleared a path through the debris to allow the truck to pass, the radio crackled to life, slicing through the heavy silence inside the pickup. Monica, her hands still gripping the wheel, leaned toward the radio on the dash, her expression tense.

"Alpha Charlie, this is Delta Three Four. We're pinned down at grid four-three-nine! Over," came the strained voice over the radio, each word hurried and laced with urgency amid the backdrop of sporadic gunfire. "Enemy forces… multiple… can't hold—"

The transmission frayed into static, and distant echoes of combat chilled the air. Monica's face hardened as she reached for the radio, her fingers trembling. "Delta Three Four, this is Alpha Charlie. What is your position? Over!" Her calm demeanor was in stark contrast to the chaos unfurling through the speaker.

But before the sentry could reply, another barrage of gunfire erupted through the radio, louder this time, the sound of war brought terrifyingly close through the tiny speaker. Then, just as suddenly, there was silence—a heavy, ominous quiet that spoke volumes.

Frank, who had rushed over and been listening intently from the driver's side window, swore under his breath and took the radio from Monica's grasp, his eyes scanning the frequency bands. "Delta Three Four. This is Alpha Two Six. Respond!" He unkeyed the mic and waited only seconds before pressing it again. "Delta Three Four. Extract to RP Bravo now! Fall back, Sam!"

Inside the truck, Ayden watched from the back seat, his jaw clenched, his mind racing with worst-case scenarios. Laney, sitting beside him, gripped his hand tightly. Her face was pale, her eyes wide as she stared at the radio.

Please, please let the sentries have heard and make it back! Ayden prayed silently. But the radio remained stubbornly silent, its static a mocking hiss against the backdrop of their desperation.

Frank slammed his fist against the side of the truck in frustration. "We have to move now," he said and then returned to finish clearing the debris. A moment later, he signaled for Monica to drive through.

Approaching the thick protective walls of New Eden, the sight that greeted them was beyond comprehension. The heavy steel gate loomed ahead, its twisted metal now a symbol of desolation rather than protection. As Monica drove past its remnants, the interior of the once-thriving compound came into view. Ayden's eyes were locked on the horizon where the medical clinic should have been, the place he'd left Clara, believing she'd be safe there.

The smoke rising in the distance filled him with dread.

Monica screeched to a halt, her hands trembling as she turned off the engine. A heavy silence enveloped them—a thick, suffocating cloak. No one moved at first, too stunned by the devastation.

Then, breaking from the trance, Laney's voice cracked through the air. "No, no, no."

As they hastily exited the truck, the sound of their footsteps echoed through the air, their feet crushing the charred remnants of what had once been their safe haven.

"My wife! My kids!" Frank sprinted toward where the bunkhouses had once stood.

Laney and Monica followed in his wake, frantic, searching for any sign of life among the rubble—for any hope someone might have survived. Ayden brought up the rear, his heart pounding in his chest, the acrid smell of burnt metal and flesh assaulting his senses. The ground was unnaturally warm under his boots.

Where the medical facility once stood, there was now only a gaping crater. The earth around it was blackened, and piles of scattered debris smoldered. The heavy-duty steel shipping container had taken a direct hit and been obliterated by the force of the explosion.

Ayden dropped to his knees in the ashes, staring into the smoke-filled crater. The heat from the hole nearly scorched his skin.

Laney collapsed beside him, her hands digging through the ash and twisted metal, her sobs piercing the heavy silence that hung over them. "The doctor, nurses, Keith, Clara…Daddy! They're all gone!"

Monica kneeled beside her. She folded her daughter in her arms, and they both howled their anguish to the skies.

Ayden froze, unable to move or process what had happened there. His sister was his only living relative. The one constant in his life through all the chaos. The hope of making it through this together was now as shattered as the ruins beneath him. He couldn't accept it. They'd been through so much to get here. She couldn't be gone—not like this!

"Clara!" Her name was a whisper on his lips. He surveyed the wreckage of what had been their last hope for safety and felt a profound emptiness. The pain of loss was sharp, a physical ache in his chest that threatened to consume him. He thought of all the plans they had made, all the promises to protect each other—and how he had failed her.

Guilt, sharp and accusing, coursed through him.

I should have never left her side.

If they'd only kept moving toward Wyoming and avoided Pennsylvania altogether, maybe she would still be alive.

Questions haunted him, each one a torment.

They sifted through the debris late into the night without finding a single survivor. As morning approached, Ayden sat on the ground amid the ashes with his head in his hands, weeping for his sister. He felt a hand on his shoulder, firm yet gentle—

"They're all gone!" Frank said. "They're dead, and we will be too if we stay here."

"Your wife? Your kids?" Ayden forced through his constricted throat.

Frank lowered his head and wiped away a tear.

Laney, her eyes red-rimmed, her face streaked with black ash and tears, stood and moved toward him.

"There's nothing left," Frank said as she took his hand. "Those bastards bombed the shit out of this place. There's nothing left here for us now. Nothing but memories turned to dust. We have to move. We have to go," he croaked, his voice hoarse with emotion.

Monica nodded, wiping her tears away with the back of her hand. "You're right." Her voice was somehow steady despite the pain that echoed in every word. "We have to keep moving. We have to get ahead of their advancement. Meet up with US forces and then bring this fight back to the Chinese. Send every one of those bastards straight to hell!"

"The roads will be crawling with PLA right now, Monica. You heard Sean's transmission. They've overrun our outposts. We need to get back to the mansion—hunker down until nightfall and then devise a plan to unass the AO."

"No! We need to hit the road now. Find the US forces," Monica said.

"That's crazy talk, Mom. Frank's right. We can't go running around without a plan. The bunker at Byers Mansion is the safest strategy right now." Laney took her mother's hand. "Please, Mom. Think of what Dad would do here."

Monica wiped away tears. She grew quiet. A moment later, she nodded. "You're right. He'd want you somewhere safe." She glanced up at Frank. "We have to get her as far away from this fighting as possible."

"Wyoming," Ayden said. "I'm going to Wyoming."

"Wyoming?" Frank's gaze shifted to the smoldering crater. "We should do a quick search for supplies. It's a long trip."

Monica's eyebrows rose. "Wyoming?"

"Wyoming!" Laney nodded, wiping tears from her cheeks.

As Ayden turned to go, suddenly, through the cloud of smoke, a figure emerged. His clothes were torn, his face smeared with soot. Ayden's mouth dropped open.

"Well, I've had better days," Mueller rasped as he approached.

Monica, Laney, and Frank turned in shock.

"Daddy!" Laney sprinted toward him and flew into his arms, nearly knocking him over.

Monica hesitated a moment. "Tyson?" She took a step toward him. "Tyson!" she cried, running to him, her hurried steps kicking up dust.

They embraced him, and Laney buried her face in his shoulder, sobbing. Monica, tears streaming down her face, clutched at Mueller as if confirming he was real.

"Where were you? We searched everywhere!" Laney asked in a rush.

"Not everywhere. After slipping out when the doc wasn't looking, I went to the cellar looking for that bottle of bourbon I hid there last summer."

"Seriously?" Monica slapped him on the shoulder.

"Ouch!" He laughed. "I figured after surviving Clairton, I deserved a drink."

Monica waved her hand over her face. "That's why you smell like a brewery."

"Well, it took me hours to get the door open. I had to drink something."

"Sure! We're out here thinking you're dead, and you were getting drunk."

"Drunk? Not yet." He held up a half-empty bottle.

Monica yanked it from his hand. "Give me that."

"Hey! That's mine!"

Frank took it from Monica, uncapped the lid, and took a drink. "Not anymore!"

Ayden would have found the exchange amusing if they weren't essentially standing in the middle of a graveyard—his sister's final resting place since he hadn't been able to find so much as a piece of her clothing.

Mueller seemed to sense Ayden's thoughts and changed the conversation.

"What's this about Wyoming?" he asked.

Monica stepped back, wiping her eyes with the back of her sleeve. "Laney and Ayden were debating heading west, away from the PLA."

Mueller's head rotated, taking in the condition of the compound. He took Monica's hand. "It's all gone—everyone?"

Monica nodded.

"Steve?" Mueller took in the spot where the communications trailer had been parked. "None of the others survived?"

Tears streamed down Monica's cheeks again. "No one but us."

"Our patrols were hit," Frank said. "The roadblocks…" He shook his head.

Mueller reached out and pulled Laney close and then wrapped an around Monica's shoulders. "We have to survive in order to fight another day." He glanced over at Ayden. "Wyoming?"

"It's the least populated state in America—and my girlfriend lives there."

Mueller studied his wife and daughter and then shifted his gaze to where the medical building once stood.

"Ty, I think we should hold up at the bunker at Byers Mansion until we know where the PLA troops are and if they've blocked the roads," Monica said.

Mueller appeared to think it over. He gripped his abdomen. "What do you think, Frank?"

"I like the idea. Once you folks are safely inside the bunker, I can do some recon and find out where the PLA troops are and see if we can avoid their patrols."

Mueller took Monica's hand in his. "Let's round up what we can salvage here and check in on Serenity and the others. I need to tell them Keith's gone. We can make a plan from there."

NINE

Tyson Mueller

New Eden Compound
Somerset Township
Washington County, Pennsylvania
Day Twenty-Two

After salvaging what they could from the compound, Ayden, Mueller, Frank, Laney, and Monica squeezed into the Ford F350 and turned it toward Byers Mansion. Tyson Mueller gazed through the window at the survival compound he and his friends had spent almost a decade planning and building. Hundreds of man-hours and hundreds of thousands of dollars, along with buckets of sweat and tears, had gone into creating a place to thrive during an apocalypse. However, in less than a minute, it had all gone up in a ball of fire, and more than thirty of his closest friends had perished. Somehow, once again, he'd survived. His wife and daughter were also spared. He'd be a fool to think they could stay and survive another attack.

Under any other scenario, Mueller would have said Ayden's plan to travel across the country to find safety was lunacy. The roads were full of their own perils, from road bandits to lack of food and supplies to interference by well-meaning government and quasi-governmental entities. The journey would be risky, but staying in Pennsylvania was no longer an option.

Laney and Ayden had argued for getting on the road straight away. Monica, still furious about the PLA destroying their home, wanted to find the military and join the fight against them. Frank, ever the voice of reason, suggested they go to ground, find out where the PLA was operating, and form a strategy to flee the area.

"We have to know where they're operating so we can avoid those areas," Frank said. "There's more than one road to Wyoming. We want a route that keeps us out of enemy hands."

Mueller's head was still fuzzy from the explosion and the meds the doctor had been giving him. He needed time to get himself together. Frank's suggestions seemed like the most prudent strategy. The last thing he wanted was to drive right into a PLA convoy and become a prisoner of war. He was too weak to survive a Chinese interrogation, and he'd do anything to keep his wife and daughter from falling into their hands. "We go to Byers Mansion, lie low for a few days, and let them think they've wiped us all out," he said.

"And then go after those bastards!" Monica spat.

"No!" Mueller placed his hand on her leg. "No, we make our way to Rory's place, stock up for the trip, and then hit the road, moving at night as much as we can."

Upon reaching the compound's destroyed checkpoint, they exited the truck, moved the lifeless bodies of their fallen sentries, laying them side by side, and then covered them with a tarp. It was the best they could do for their friends. Back in the vehicle, no one spoke, each dwelling in their own grief over the ones they'd lost.

Ayden wore a blank expression, staring out his side window.

Mueller felt incredibly blessed to still have his wife and daughter, but he was acutely aware of life's fragility and how he could lose everything in an instant.

As the Ford F350 crested the last hill before Byers Mansion, Tyson Mueller braced himself, his gaze fixed on the horizon where black smoke billowed into the sky, a dark column marking the mansion's location. The sight that unfolded as they approached was a grim tableau of destruction, one that struck Mueller with a chilling sense of déjà vu.

Once a symbol of opulence and rich history, Byers Mansion now lay in ruins, reduced to a smoldering heap of debris. Its blackened frame had collapsed in on itself, while the stables were no more than charred remains.

From the back seat of the truck, Mueller's eyes scanned the wreckage. Scorched earth surrounded what was left of the mansion, and the overgrown ornate gardens were now just ash and debris. Lingering small fires still burned, feeding on stubborn remnants. It was clear the drone strike had not only aimed to obliterate the mansion but also to ensure nothing salvageable was left.

Mueller's heart sank as he envisioned the panicked moments before the strike; the futile attempts of those who might have tried to escape the inferno. The reality of their war-torn world hit him anew. Nowhere was safe, no stronghold secure enough in the face of the technological might of enemy drones.

Beside him, Monica clutched his hand, her face pale and her lips pressed into a thin line. The loss of their own compound was a fresh wound, and the sight of the mansion in ruins only intensified the pain. Her eyes, usually so full of fire and determination, now mirrored the despair that had settled over the group.

Laney wrung her hands, muttering to herself, "It's all gone… everything's gone."

After maneuvering the truck close to the remains, Frank suggested they stash it under cover to avoid drawing any attention. They camouflaged the pickup with broken limbs and branches from the nearby woods, masking its presence in the shadow of the destroyed mansion.

Once they had concealed the truck, Mueller led the group to the backyard. The air reeked of smoke and burnt wood, a pungent reminder of the ferocity of the attack. His gaze swept over the charred landscape before settling on a pile of wood near what used to be the garden. He walked over to an innocuous patch of earth beside the pile and rapped on what appeared to be solid ground. The dull thud of his knuckles against metal hinted at the hatch beneath.

"Hello down there! It's Tyson Mueller," he called out, his voice echoing slightly against the metal hatch.

A few tense moments passed before the hatch creaked open to reveal Tanner, one of Hugh Meecham's sons. Relief washed over his face as he recognized Mueller and motioned them inside.

One by one, Ayden, Monica, Laney, Frank, and Mueller descended the narrow steps into the bunker. The air inside was stale, thick with the anxiety of its already overcrowded occupants. Similar to WWII air raid shelters, the bunker seemed out of place in rural western Pennsylvania.

As the last of them entered, Serenity rose to her feet, clutching her abdomen where the shrapnel wound still ached. Her face was pale, her eyes red-rimmed and hollow. She looked past the descending figures, as if searching the shadows for her father, confusion etched into her features. The dim light from a battery-operated lantern perched on a stack of crates cast long, flickering shadows, adding to the surreal, disorienting atmosphere.

"Dad?" Serenity's voice was a broken whisper, her eyes darting from face to face. Her pained expression evidence she hadn't found the one she sought.

Mueller's heart clenched as he watched her, the depth of her grief and confusion evident in her face. He had promised safety, yet here they were, broken and lost. He felt the guilt wash over him anew, a relentless tide that threatened to drown him.

Mueller broke the solemn silence. "Our compound was hit as well—obliterated. There's nothing left."

"Serenity," Sadie said gently, stepping forward and placing a hand on the young woman's shoulder. "Come, sit down. Let's rest for a moment."

But Serenity didn't move, her eyes still scanning the bunker's dim interior. "Where is he?" she asked, her voice trembling. "Where's my dad?"

Mueller stepped closer, his own heart heavy with the knowledge of the truth. "Serenity," he began, his voice thick with emotion. "Keith... he didn't make it."

The words hung in the air, heavy and final. Serenity's knees buckled slightly, but Sadie caught her. She looked at Mueller, the pain in her gaze piercing through him. "No," she whispered. "No, he can't be gone."

Mueller's throat tightened, and he felt tears sting his eyes. He reached out, but Serenity stepped back, wrapping her arms around herself as if trying to hold in the pieces of her broken heart.

Sadie guided Serenity to a nearby crate, easing her down gently. Laney sat beside her, taking her hand in silent support. Frank, his own expression somber, leaned against the wall, the weight of their shared loss evident in his posture.

Mueller took a deep breath, trying to steady himself. His own grief not overwhelming.

Serenity lifted her head, tears streaming down her face. She met Mueller's eyes as if still not ready to accept her loss.

The grief etched into her features was a knife to Mueller's heart. He had rescued her father from the PLA in Clairton, only to fail in keeping him safe at his own compound. He felt responsible, as if he had personally let them all down. The guilt was overwhelming, a relentless weight on his soul.

Mueller lowered himself onto a stack of crates and hung his head. No one spoke for a long time. Quiet sobs could be heard from the group as they each grieved their losses.

Frank, with his back against the hatch door, finally broke the silence. He outlined their intention to find safety far from the current hot zones of conflict. "I know we're all hurting, but we really need to discuss our next steps. We can't remain down here forever."

Everyone looked up.

Serenity wiped tears from her face. "You're right. We don't have time for this. We need to figure out how to keep the rest of us alive."

"We're planning to head to Wyoming," Ayden said.

Tanner rubbed his chin. "We've been thinking of Mexico. Might be safer down south, away from the main conflict areas."

The bunker fell silent as those present considered the two vastly different strategies. Mueller exchanged a long look with Laney and Monica, gauging their reactions to the options laid out before them. The decision was critical, each path fraught with its own set of dangers and uncertainties. "We need to think this through," Mueller said, turning to address the group as a whole. "Let's weigh the risks and decide together. We can split up based on what each of us feels is best for our families."

Monica nodded in agreement, her eyes meeting Mueller's. "We need a plan that keeps us safe but also moving. Staying hidden isn't a long-term solution."

Frank took a seat on a crate. "Let's lay out everything tonight. Routes, supplies, potential dangers, and then decide. We need a solid plan if we're to make it through this."

TEN

Ayden

Byers Mansion Bunker
Bowers Township
Washington County, Pennsylvania
Day Twenty-Two

Within the bunker's dim light, Ayden listened in silence as Tanner laid out his argument for heading to Mexico. As the planning session progressed, it almost seemed Ayden would be traveling alone to Wyoming. The air was thick, filled with the earthy scent of damp concrete and the underlying tension of decisions that could mean life or death. Ayden's gaze drifted from face to face, each one marked by the strain of recent losses and the weight of impending choices.

"Think about it," Tanner urged, his voice earnest as he addressed the group. "The US is a war zone right now. Heading to Wyoming... we're just moving from one battle-ridden state to another. Mexico offers neutrality, a chance to really get away from the conflict."

Laney nervously rubbed her hands on her dirt-caked cargo

pants. "But what about the journey there? We know the risks here —the devil you know versus the devil you don't."

Finn rose and moved over by Ayden, who helped him climb onto a nearby crate. The kid didn't appear all that fazed by what had happened. Ayden smiled down at him as Tanner responded.

"That's true. The road to Mexico won't be easy. We'll have to pass through several states, each with its own challenges. There are road bandits, displaced civilians, not to mention the scattered PLA forces and American military checkpoints."

"And once we get to the Mexican border, what then?" Frank twisted the wedding ring on his finger. "We won't be the only ones fleeing the war. Refugees from all over the United States will overwhelm the Mexican government. The infrastructure will be strained."

Monica leaned forward. "And let's not forget, they might not welcome us. There's a real possibility of internment camps and restrictions on movement. The Mexican government has been tightening its borders to manage the influx."

Ayden felt a knot form in his stomach as he considered the potential realities of their situation upon reaching Mexico. The thought of fleeing from one uncertain situation into another was daunting. He imagined arriving in a foreign land, only to be confined and stripped of the freedom they so desperately sought.

Mueller crossed his arms over his chest and leaned back against the wall of the bunker. "If we make it to Mexico and they let us in, we also have to consider how we'd live. Most of us don't speak Spanish—"

Tanner interrupted him. "Mexico has communities of American expats. We could find support networks, maybe even some semblance of normalcy. And being so far from the frontline might give us a real chance at a peaceful life."

"Yeah, but we have limited funds, and finding work in a saturated refugee market would be tough," Mueller continued.

"Well…" Serenity said, smiling. "That's not exactly true."

"You're right." Sadie turned to face her. "But how would we haul it all there?"

Ayden had no idea what they were talking about.

Finn leaned close and whispered in his ear, "They're talking about the buried treasure we found in the stables."

Ayden stared at him wide-eyed. "Buried treasure?"

A broad grin spread across Finn's face. His sandy brown hair flopped as he nodded. "Yep! Gold coins—lots of them."

"Gold?" Mueller asked with his eyebrows raised.

Sadie nodded, her grin broadening. "We've got like half a million dollars in gold coins buried in our woods."

"Craig Hall's gold," Serenity added.

The revelation hung in the air as everyone digested this new information. The introduction of this resource had a profound impact on the dynamics of their discussion. Suddenly, the possibility of funding their journey, perhaps even securing a stable start in Mexico, seemed within reach.

The group fell silent.

Ayden felt a wave of conflicting emotions. While the others pondered the logistics and safety of retrieving and transporting the gold, his mind was elsewhere. The lure of escaping the immediate dangers of war by heading to Mexico was strong, yet the myriad of uncertainties of refugee life there were daunting. Moreover, Ayden couldn't help but think of Mia and the boys back in Farson. He couldn't imagine going on with his life without knowing their fate. Once he reached the Christiansens' ranch and reunited with them, they might consider making the trek to Mexico later if things deteriorated further. Perhaps they might even find this group again there.

Monica repositioned herself on the crate. "We could use the gold to help us settle, maybe even start a business to sustain ourselves. But we need a solid plan for security. We're talking about a lot of money in an unstable situation. We could attract the wrong kind of attention." She glanced over at Frank with a questioning expression.

"You're right. The gold could change our circumstances, sure, but it also paints a massive target on our backs," he said. "We need to think this through, not just about getting to Mexico, but what happens when we arrive? How do we protect ourselves and the gold? How do we integrate into a new society where we're seen as wealthy foreigners?"

Mueller shook his head. "I don't know. Let's not forget the political aspect, either. Mexico's government is already overwhelmed with refugees. How will they react to a group like ours arriving with significant wealth?"

"And then there's crossing into Mexico legally. What do we do if we're turned away at the border? Or worse, what if they let us in, but then we're detained or restricted to a certain area because we're refugees?" Laney asked.

Tanner waved his hand in the air. "But if we make it, and if we manage it right, settling in Mexico could offer us a real chance to start over. We could find a place away from the war, maybe even out of reach of the global conflict."

"And even with the funds, the journey and what awaits us there in Mexico comes with its own set of challenges," Mueller said.

The group appeared to take his words seriously, the initial excitement about the gold tempered by the reality of the risks involved. Ayden was still unconvinced. The discussion deepened as they began to tackle the specifics of transporting the gold, a topic that introduced a new level of complexity to their planning.

Frank leaned back against the bunker's cool wall, folding his arms as he stared up at the bunker's ceiling. "First things first: retrieving the gold safely. We need to be stealthy and avoid any unnecessary attention. How do we even transport it? A monster box of gold isn't easy to hide."

Serenity undid her ponytail and shook out her hair. She and Tanner briefly made eye contact. "We could divide it among several backpacks. Spread the weight and the risk. If one of us gets caught, it doesn't compromise the entire stash."

"And converting it into something more liquid before hitting the border is crucial." Monica bobbed her head. "We can't show up in Mexico with a box of gold and not expect to draw attention. Maybe we can find a broker or a trustworthy contact who could help us exchange some of it for pesos or other tradeable assets."

"We should only convert a small portion before we leave," Mueller said. "Keep the rest secure until we know who we can trust." He grew quiet for a moment as he picked at the ash-covered bandage on his left arm. "Then there's also the journey itself to consider. The roads aren't just highways; they're more like gauntlets now. Between here and Mexico, there are countless dangers. We need to be prepared for everything from PLA check-points to rogue militias and everything in between."

Ayden's heart raced at the thought of stumbling into a PLA checkpoint. They would face capture or worse—death. The terrifying possibility of capture conjured images of brutal interrogations followed by a grim fate in a detention camp, much like the horrifying accounts of Uyghurs and other ethnic minorities confined in China's so-called vocational education and training centers. These centers, notorious for their harrowing conditions under the guise of combating extremism and fostering social integration, represented a living nightmare.

Clara had always expressed a deep fear of such a fate, her voice trembling whenever the topic arose. Now, as Ayden envisioned the stark reality of their situation, a profound sense of dread overwhelmed him. He squeezed his eyes shut, trying to block out the haunting images, but the sharp pang of grief clutched at his chest, tightening like a vise. Each breath became a struggle against the weight of his fears and the unbearable loss of Clara, whose fears had now become his own haunting reality.

ELEVEN

Mia

Christiansen Ranch
Farson, Wyoming
Day Twenty-Two

The front door swung open with a resounding thud as Carter burst through, his voice brimming with urgency. "Helen's coming down the driveway!"

"Is she alone?" Mia asked, her eyes darting to the window.

"No, she's with Bill."

"Go tell Grammy; she's out back hanging laundry."

"Yes, ma'am," Carter replied, his footsteps fading as he disappeared through the kitchen door.

Mia stepped onto the porch just as Helen and her husband rounded into view, pedaling their bicycles up the gravel path. The front basket on Helen's bike was brimming with fresh vegetables.

"Hey there, neighbor!" Bill called out, raising his hand in greeting as he came to a halt. "Is your dad around?"

"He's in the barn, I think." Mia nodded toward the large structure in the distance.

As Bill headed toward the barn, Helen approached the porch, dismounting with a friendly smile. "I brought you some squash," she announced, lifting a bag from her basket. "Planned to take it to Rock Springs, but I figured you might want some."

"Rock Springs?" Mia echoed, accepting the vegetables with a curious tilt of her head.

"Market Days!" Helen exclaimed, her eyes twinkling with excitement. "It's like a swap meet or farmer's market where people trade what they have. You haven't heard?"

"No," Mia admitted, intrigued.

"With the Russians in the area occupied by our US forces, an open air market popped up in Rock Springs with people gathering there to trade goods and services.

Mia raised her eyebrows. "What kind of things do they have there?"

"Oh, all sorts. Hand tools that don't require power, handmade soaps, and even bullets. Bullets are worth their weight in gold there. If you've got bullets, you can trade for just about anything."

"And beef?" Mia queried, her gaze drifting toward the pasture where their cattle grazed.

Helen shook her head. "Most folks are holding onto their cattle tight. But firewood, now that's in demand. One guy had loads of it last time, but his asking price was more than we could afford. Didn't want veggies for it, that's for sure."

Mia pondered the potential trade, her mind racing with the possibilities. "We're desperate for firewood, and we've got the beef if it could get us a good stockpile."

"Hello, Helen!" Melody's voice rang out as she rounded the corner of the house, wiping her hands on her apron. "Good to see you!"

As Helen and Melody disappeared inside to catch up, Mia found Dirk, the ranch manager, and relayed the idea of trading at the market. "The biggest issue will be keeping the meat cool once it's butchered."

"What if we butchered it right at the market?" Mia suggested. "Whoever trades with us could handle the cooling."

Dirk nodded, rubbing his chin thoughtfully. "Messy but doable."

"Let me talk it over with Dad. In the meantime, can you select a couple of steers for us to take?"

"Will do, Ms. Mia." Dirk pulled on his leather gloves. "I'll leave most of the cowboys here for security, though."

"That's between you and Dad. Just let them know they're valued, whether they go or stay," Mia said, watching Dirk head toward the pasture.

That evening, gathered around the dinner table, the family discussed their strategy for the market. "If we can trade some steers for a substantial supply of wood and other essentials, it might just see us through the winter," Mia proposed.

"We should also look for medical supplies and warmer clothes for the kids," Melody added, nodding in agreement.

The prospect of engaging with the broader community at Rock Springs offered a flicker of hope, an echo of normalcy amidst the chaos of war. They discussed establishing regular trades, even securing luxury items like honey that were rare in their isolated condition.

Watching her sons play outside later, with the youngest occasionally scanning the road as if waiting for someone, Mia felt a mix of dread and resolve. Preparing for the journey to Rock Springs wasn't just about trading—it was about connecting with others, assessing the resilience and unity of their wider community, and bracing for the long, uncertain winter ahead.

TWELVE

Ayden

Byers Mansion Bunker
Bowers Township
Washington County, Pennsylvania
Day Twenty-Three

Ayden's eyes grew heavy as he listened to the others' strategies about their trip to Mexico. His mind drifted, overwhelmed by the prospect of traveling to Wyoming alone. Maybe it was better that way. He'd only have himself to worry about.

"We should drive straight through, taking turns at the wheel," Mueller said. "We'll stick to back roads where there's less PLA presence."

Frank lifted an eyebrow. "But those routes come with their own problems—less reliable roads, the potential for getting lost without proper navigation, and community roadblocks like those we erected." His brows knitted together. "Not to mention the state of the roads. Some of those routes could be bombed out or blocked. We'll need alternative paths planned, maybe even some off-roading. Do we have maps that are detailed enough for that?"

"I don't," Tanner said.

Frank leaned forward with his arms crossed. "Information is key. We'll need real-time intel on what areas to avoid. That means keeping in touch with any friendly forces or local contacts we can trust. Maybe even scouting ahead when possible."

"Or we stick closer to main routes but travel at night like we discussed earlier," Mueller said. "Those would come with more risk from patrols, but the roads are better, and if we're careful, we can move faster."

Ayden recalled the military convoys he'd encountered on his way to Harpers Ferry—the one with the huge vehicle that had scooped up cars, trucks, and vans, shoving them to the sides of the road like newly fallen snow.

"And it's not just about getting through checkpoints or dodging militias," Frank said. "Whatever route we choose, we're going to have to stop eventually to find fuel, food, water. Every stop has the potential for confrontation." Frank glanced over at Finn and then at the baby in Liz's arms. "No matter what route we take, our biggest danger will be people—road bandits preying on refugees or groups like us—people just trying to survive."

Mueller bobbed his head. "True. We have to be ready for inter-actions with civilians. Not everyone out there is a threat, but desperate people can be unpredictable. We'll need to decide how to handle those situations—when to help and when to keep moving."

"It sounds like whatever route we choose, the path is fraught with challenges," Laney said. "I agree with Frank. We need to consider all these points and draft up a few potential travel plans, each with its own set of contingencies."

"Then it's settled. We prepare as best we can." Tanner made eye contact with Mueller. "We secure the gold, plan our routes, and make our way to what we hope will be safer ground."

"I'm not sure about Mexico," Serenity said. She pressed her fingers to her lips. "I'm not all that comfortable leaving my coun-try. I'd like to at least consider going to Wyoming."

Ayden sat up straighter.

Frank met Serenity's gaze. He studied her for a moment. "Wyoming has its advantages." He looked around the bunker. "First, it's familiar territory. We speak the language. We somewhat know the landscape, and we would have our network of contacts that might still be operational. Wyoming's diverse terrain, including the Black Hills, the Great Plains, the Southern, Middle, and Northern Rocky Mountains, and the Wyoming Basin, would make it difficult for the PLA to occupy and provide us with plenty of places to hide if they tried."

Ayden readied himself to make his case for everyone to join him and head to Wyoming. "You're right, Frank. There are no major metropolitan areas, and the state's two largest urban areas, Casper and Cheyenne, are really just small cities. The landscape mostly consists of large expanses of wide-open spaces filled with ranches and farms." Ayden took a moment to catch his breath. "You'd have no problem finding a place to settle and sufficient resources to survive." He smiled broadly. "The locals are rugged and adaptable people, used to hardships."

Frank stifled a yawn and crossed his ankles. "It's not just about geography, Ayden. Wyoming seems to be far from the major conflict zones that are seeing the heaviest PLA activity. The state could offer us the potential to rebuild and establish a secure base away from the front lines. We could find other survivor groups and maybe even coordinate with parts of the US military that are regrouping there."

The mood in the room shifted again, a renewed flicker of hope found in Frank's and Ayden's words. However, Mueller, leaning against the cold concrete wall, folded his arms and sighed. "But let's not overlook the dangers. Wyoming might be away from the front lines, but it's also isolated. That means long supply lines, potential scarcity of resources, and brutal winters that could lock us down for months. We would be exposed during our travel there, and if caught, it would be in a place where support could be miles away."

Tanner raked his hand through his hair. "We also have to think about the long term. Even if we make it to Wyoming, what then?" He let his hand fall to his lap. "We're assuming it's safe and that we can rebuild there. But we don't know the current situation on the ground."

"It sounds risky either way, but at least Wyoming doesn't put us directly in a new political landscape with uncertain laws and potential hostility toward refugees," Monica said.

"That's a valid point," Mueller said. "If we proceed on a route toward Wyoming, we need to be able to pivot—perhaps even reconsider Mexico or another location if things on the ground change."

"We need a solid exit strategy for either option," Frank said. "If we go to Mexico, we need contingency plans for being turned away at the border or worse. If we head to Wyoming, we need to be prepared for ongoing conflict, maybe even a harsh winter."

The group nodded in agreement.

Tanner fixed his gaze on Serenity. "I understand why some would choose Wyoming, but…" He shifted his gaze to his brother, Danny. "We're still heading to Mexico."

Serenity leaned forward, winced from the movement, and took her mother's hand. "I don't like the idea of running to a foreign country. We can't know that things would be any better there than in Wyoming. What do you think?"

"I don't know." Sadie shifted in her seat. "Jane? Geneva? What about you?"

"Puerto Vallarta or Mérida are great. There are a lot of expats there. It's warm and beautiful," Geneva said.

"Lake Chapala area has the largest concentration of expats." Jane took her grandson's hand. "As nice as those areas were before all this, things will have definitely changed by now with a flood of refugees crossing their border, most arriving with nothing. We can't say we'd even make it to those places. There are so many unknowns." She smoothed back a strand of her gray hair and sighed.

"I'd prefer Wyoming," Finn said, his voice tinged with sadness. "I've always wanted to see Yellowstone. Mom promised me we'd go someday."

Jane's eyes glistened as she wrapped her arm around him and kissed him on top of his head.

"Mom wanted to take me to see the Yermo xanthocephalus." He smiled up at Ayden. "My mom owned a flower shop in East Dentonville. It burned down right after my dad killed her," he said with sadness in his tone.

Jane wiped away tears as he continued.

"The Yermo is a one of a kind plant. It is a member of the sunflower or daisy family and only grows in two places in the middle of Wyoming. Botanists say this plant might be very new or very old, and it's not like its plant cousins that live far away."

Ayden leaned forward. "I'm very sorry about your mother, Finn. If we go to Wyoming, I bet my girlfriend, Mia, would love to take you and her three sons to see this Yermo flower."

"How old are her sons?" Finn asked.

"Carter is nine. Luke is seven, and Xavier is four."

Finn's eyes lit up. He slid down from his position next to his grandmother and Serenity and moved closer to Ayden. "You're not their daddy?"

"No."

"Where is he?"

"Well, he died."

Finn was quiet for a moment.

"Are you their stepfather?"

"No, Mia and I aren't married."

"Are you going to marry their mom so you can be their dad?"

Ayden glanced around the room as he thought about his question. He had planned to talk to Mia about their relationship the day before the EMP attack. Ayden didn't know if she'd ever considered a future with him. He had to consider the possibility that he'd make it all the way to Wyoming to learn her feelings for him didn't run that deep.

"I intend to marry her if she'll have me," he said, finally. But first, he'd need to survive a trip across the country to reach her.

"So," Laney said. "Who besides Ayden is going to Wyoming, and who is heading to Mexico?"

"My family and I are going to Mexico. You're all welcome to join us," Tanner said.

"Show of hands for Mexico," Danny said.

Geneva and Liz raised their hands.

"I'd like to take Leah," Liz said. "I believe her mother would have wanted her to go to Mexico."

Sadie glared at Liz and then took Jacob's hand. "Jacob, Serenity, and I are going to Wyoming. Right, Renny?"

"Right." Serenity wore a pained expression. "You should come with us, Liz. Rick would want his sons to stay together."

Liz shot to her feet, nearly bumping her head on the bunker's low ceiling. "Rick isn't here. William is my son, and I have to do what is right for him! I'm going with Tanner and his family."

"It's okay," Jacob said. "We'll come to visit after things get better here in the States."

Serenity gave him a reassuring smile. "Yeah, we can visit sometime."

"Who else will be going with us?" Tanner asked. "Jane?"

Jane compressed her lips and rubbed her deceased daughter's pendant between her fingers. "Finn and I are going to Wyoming."

"Yippee!" Finn said. "And Gunner?"

"And Gunner." She smiled down at the boy.

Frank gathered up his rifle and stood. "I'm an American. I'm not abandoning my nation. After I help you folks reach Wyoming, I intend to find a group of resistance fighters to take back our country."

"I'm going with you," Laney said, moving to his side. "I want to help Ayden reach his loved ones as he helped me."

Mueller chuckled and wrapped his arm around Monica's shoulders. "Well, hell, I guess that means you and I are going to Wyoming."

"I count eight adults, two children, and a dog for Wyoming," Frank said. "That's a lot of people to fit in our truck, especially with the gear and supplies we were able to salvage from the compound."

"We'll make room for everyone in the pickup's bed," Laney said. "We can move stuff around, and I can ride back there."

Serenity braced herself on a nearby box and stood. "Jacob and I can ride in the bed with you."

Sadie shook her head. "No, Serenity. It will be too painful for you."

"She's right, Serenity," Ayden said. "I'll ride back there. You take the back seat."

"Let me ride in the bed, too," Sadie added. "It'll give you more room, baby girl."

"We'll pile in and see how it goes, then." Frank now had a broad grin on his face.

Ayden felt a surge of excitement rise within him. "When do we leave?"

"As soon as we scope things out and find out if the PLA has left the area," Frank said. "Let's get to it!"

THIRTEEN

Serenity

Byers Mansion
Bowers Township
Washington County, Pennsylvania
Day Twenty-Three

Frank, Tanner, and Ayden grabbed their rifles and lined up at the hatch door. Tanner popped the hatch, peered out, then crept out of the hole, followed by Ayden. Mueller was just about to ascend the steps when Frank threw an arm across his chest and stopped him.

"You should stay here. Let us check it out. You've been shot and blown up twice. You'll just slow me down," Frank said.

Mueller hesitated a moment before he complied, and Frank continued up the steps and shut the hatch.

The occupants of the bunker sat in silence, waiting.

"It's been fifteen minutes already," Finn informed them, pointing to the oversized watch on his wrist. "It was Grandpa Jim's." He glanced up at Jane. "I hope you don't mind I took it. I wanted something to remember him by."

Serenity's stomach tightened as she recalled how she'd watched Jim get gunned down in their battle with Walt Cayman's crew. Maria and Raul had lost their daughter, Isabella. Serenity held her breath a moment, suppressing tears. They were all gone now. The people hiding in this bunker were the only survivors. Serenity was torn apart by the cruel irony that she had been separated from her father for years while he was in prison, and now, just as they had finally been reunited, he was killed in the PLA drone strike. She should have stayed. Maybe she could have done something to save him. Tears slid down her cheeks, unchecked and unstoppable. The pain of their brief reunion, followed by such a swift, cruel loss, was unbearable. They all had so much grieving to do, but there was no time for such things now—survival demanded every ounce of their time and energy, leaving no room for the sorrow that threatened to engulf them all.

Jane nodded. "I'm sure Grandpa Jim would have wanted you to have his watch, Finn." She reached beneath the collar of her shirt, pulled out a pendant, and smiled. "This was your mother's."

Finn smiled, and then his face turned serious. "It was her favorite."

"Because you gave it to her."

The bunker grew quiet, and Serenity stared at the hatch, willing it to open so they could get on the road. She wanted to put Pennsylvania and all its painful memories behind her. Two hours passed before the hatch opened. When it did, Danny jumped to his feet, shouldering his rifle.

"Don't shoot!" Frank called down. "It's just us."

"Is it clear?" Serenity asked, rising slowly and heading over to the steps.

"For now. Team Wyoming, grab your stuff and let's go. We've moved the truck from the woods to the driveway."

Jane ran a length of rope under Gunner's collar and handed it to Frank. He led the beagle out of the bunker as Jane and Finn climbed out behind him. Finn held tightly to the leash while they said their goodbyes to the Mexico-bound group.

Serenity wrapped her arm around Tanner's neck. "I'm going to miss you. Thank you for everything you've done for me and my family."

"I'm going to miss you, too. You take care of yourself, Serenity."

She quickly hugged Danny, Geneva, and the others, and then Ayden helped her climb into the pickup's back passenger seat while Jacob hugged Liz and his little brother.

After Ayden closed her door and stepped back, Tanner and Danny drew near. Tanner stuck out his hand, and they bumped their fists.

"Adios, Meechams," Serenity said. "Thanks for looking out for Jacob's stepmom and little brother, Tanner."

"Yeah, no problem."

Serenity snickered. He didn't know Liz. But he was about to find out what a pain in the butt she could be.

Frank chopped the air and opened the back driver's side door for Jane. She scooted over beside Serenity. "Let's roll out, people."

"Where are Gunner and I going to ride?" Finn asked. "What about in the back with Ayden?"

Frank stopped with one leg in the truck. He looked at Jane.

"I suppose so, but don't stand up while we're moving."

"Yes, ma'am," Finn called, climbing down from the vehicle.

Ayden followed them around to the back of the truck, lifted the beagle onto the tailgate, and then he and Finn climbed over the tailgate and into the truck's bed. The engine started, and the pick-up's headlights illuminated the Mexico-bound group. Liz and Geneva waved as the Ford pulled down the driveway.

Serenity fought the urge to look out the passenger window as they drove past what had been their stables. The fences in the front pastures that lined the driveway were down, posts across the gravel drive. Frank drove the truck around them until they reached the gate. The large ornate gate was lying on the opposite side of the road.

Laney's, Finn's, and Jacob's voices wafted through the sliding rear window. Serenity couldn't see them in the darkness, but she could imagine Jacob talking with his hands flailing, as usual. Within minutes, they were pulling onto Highway 136 and heading west. Serenity was surprised there weren't stalled cars blocking the road. She did see one or two off in ditches, but the streets were all drivable. The few houses they passed were dark. But there were a couple of lights in barns and shops along the way.

Two hours later, they finally managed to cross the Pennsylvania-West Virginia state lines and were approaching the river town of Moundsville, West Virginia. Frank pulled over onto the shoulder and clicked off the headlights. He turned and knocked on the back glass, and seconds later, Ayden's face appeared in the driver's side window.

"We're coming up on a town just around that bend in the road ahead. I need you to take the wheel while Laney and I scout ahead and check it out." He opened his driver's side door, and Serenity noted the inside dome light didn't come on. She wondered if it was broken already or if Frank had had the forethought to disable it for the trip.

"Take my night vision goggles with you," Mueller said, handing him the NVGs.

Serenity heard boots hit the gravel, and then Frank and Laney disappeared from view.

Several minutes passed, and then, out of nowhere, they reappeared in Ayden's window—rifles slung across their chests.

"Roadblock about a mile ahead. Two guards, but the road is blocked with cars and an ambulance." Laney handed Ayden the NVGs.

"That sucks!" Monica said from her position between Ayden and Mueller in the front seat.

"Okay, we knew we'd run into barricaded towns sooner or later." Mueller leant over her.

"Do we go around or try to talk our way through?"

"They might let us through if we tell them we're heading west," Ayden said.

"Or they could detain us and take our truck," Frank groused.

Mueller nodded. "Yeah, there's that."

"Let's not risk it. We can find a way around." Laney suggested.

Monica flicked on a flashlight. "We could, but we have to cross the Ohio River." She checked the map in her lap. "But the next bridge we could take is thirty miles south at New Martinsville."

"Let's do that," Mueller said, leaning toward the map. "We can head south and cross the Ohio River at Blennerhassett."

Once Ayden and Laney had climbed back into the bed of the pickup, Frank pulled the truck back on the road. Serenity glanced back to check on her mother and brother; she couldn't see them, but she could hear Finn talking Jacob's ear off about something. The kid sounded excited, but Jacob had begun responding with one-word answers. Serenity wondered if that was because he was concerned about their trip or about his stepmother and little brother.

Frank made a series of turns to avoid potential roadblocks before taking a highway heading south. Soon, they were skirting a town and turning onto the road that approached the bridge over the Ohio River. Frank slowed the pickup and pulled to the shoulder. He shut off the headlights and then leaned out the open driver's window.

"What's going on?" Laney asked.

"I need you and Ayden."

Ayden and Laney jumped down and stood next to the driver's door. Pulling the NVGs from the dash, Frank opened the driver's door.

"Ayden, climb in. Laney, come with me."

"What's going on?" Serenity asked, leaning forward in her seat. She could see nothing in the darkness.

Frank ignored her question as Ayden climbed in behind the wheel.

"What's up? What did you see, Frank?" Mueller asked, shifting in his seat.

"Just movement from one side of the road to the other. The bridge is a perfect ambush point." He slid the NVGs over his head, and he and Laney moved out of sight with their rifles shouldered.

"No lights. No sound," Mueller said as he watched them disappear. "Tell the folks in the back."

Serenity opened the sliding window and repeated what Mueller had told her. She wondered if Jacob was as afraid as she was. Serenity knew her baby brother would never admit to it if he were.

Gunner barked and whined, and they all shushed him quietly. Serenity was worried he might give away their position and get them all killed.

A moment later, gunfire erupted from the end of the bridge. Serenity and Jane both ducked down in their seats the best they could. Serenity felt the staples in her abdomen pull against her skin.

The shooting only lasted a minute, but it felt like an eternity before Frank and Laney returned. Frank flung open the driver's door and hustled Ayden out of the truck. He slid back into the cab and shut the door. Serenity and Jane sat up as Laney and Ayden ran around to the back.

"Frank, is everything okay?" Serenity asked.

"Yeah, it's fine. You mind handing me a couple of wet wipes, Monica?" Frank asked.

Monica fished the packet off the floor between her feet, pulled out a handful, and handed them to Frank. He wiped his hands and threw the towelettes out the truck window.

"That's littering!" Monica said.

"Not now, Monica," Mueller gritted.

Frank started the truck and crawled across the bridge into Ohio. On the other side, he sped up. Moments later, they navigated past an industrial area, turned onto a two-lane road, and then moved through a more rural area.

"What happened back there, Frank?" Serenity asked. "Was it the PLA?"

"No."

"Road bandits?" Monica asked.

"I don't know what you call them. They must have had lookouts somewhere, and when they saw us coming, thought they'd ambush us—take our stuff and the truck."

"One stuck me with a knife. The blade caught me between the fingers. Stings like a..." He trailed off.

"It's harder to spot them in the dark," Monica said.

"That's why everyone needs to have their heads on a swivel. Call out if you see anything," Mueller said.

A couple of miles later, Frank barely slowed, making a right turn onto another road, causing Jane and Serenity to slide across the back seat. Jane moaned.

"Are you all right, Jane?" Serenity asked.

"Yeah, just a little sore."

"Aren't we all," Mueller said.

"We've been through a lot," Jane said.

"Pfft. You can say that!" Serenity had been kidnapped, beaten, zip-tied, chased down, and shot in the last three weeks, and every muscle in her body bore testament to it. She felt like she hadn't slept in months.

"Are we going to try to drive straight through to Wyoming without stopping to sleep?" Serenity asked, breaking the silence.

"No," Mueller said. "We need intel. We need to find out what we're heading into."

"Where are we going, then?"

"To a friend's place near Chillicothe, Ohio," Mueller said.

"Who is that?" Monica asked.

"Wiley and Roadrunner."

"They're in Chillicothe? I didn't know that."

"How far is it to this friend's house?" Jane asked.

"Taking the back roads—about four or five hours. We should be there by morning."

FOURTEEN

Serenity

Highway 339
Blennerhassett, Ohio
Day Twenty-Three

The headlights sliced through the vast emptiness of the endless road, flanked by unbroken rows of trees that occasionally parted to reveal farmhouses, barns, and shops. The road snaked ahead, its curves and dips sending waves of nausea through her body. With every blind curve, Serenity's muscles tensed, bracing for unseen dangers.

"I think I'm going to be sick," she managed, her hand working the window crank to let in some fresh air.

"She's carsick, Frank," Monica said. "Try to ease up on those curves."

Frank eased off the accelerator. "Sorry."

"We might also want to take it slow to avoid deer or an unexpected roadblock," Mueller said.

"Are the roads like this the whole way?" The wind whipped Serenity's ponytail as she took deep breaths of fresh air.

"Pretty much. Highway 50 would be straighter, but we can't risk major roads. We're more likely to run into the PLA."

Mueller explained his plan to stay on back roads and zigzag around towns and villages.

After driving north for about ten miles, they turned left, just past the post office in Cutler, Ohio, and headed west. A few miles later, headlights of multiple vehicles appeared ahead of them, coming their way.

Frank cut his lights in a flash and pulled into the next driveway, which circled an old barn. He parked next to it and shut off the engine. Frank and Ayden jumped out, and Mueller grabbed his rifle. Serenity turned in the seat and watched the approaching lights. When they passed the driveway, Serenity exhaled the breath she was holding.

A moment later, Frank, Ayden, and Laney appeared.

"Looked like sheriff vehicles—heading somewhere fast," Laney said.

"They didn't see us?" Mueller asked.

"They had to have seen our headlights, but they didn't even slow down to check us out," Ayden said.

"I think we should continue on. We can't stay here and wait for them to return," Frank said, scanning the area.

Frank started the truck and took them back onto the roadway. He waited a few seconds, then sped up down the county road, heading west. A roadblock in the city of Aspen, Ohio, sent them north before turning onto Highway 56 and heading west again. They encountered no trouble at New Plymouth and slipped in and out of town.

Thirty minutes later, after crossing a small bridge near Tar Hollow State Park, Frank turned off the engine. Mueller opened his door and stepped out with the NVGs in his hands.

"See anything?" Monica asked.

"There's a roadblock just past that—"

"Get those hands in the air, mister!" a voice yelled in the dark.

"Rory! Rory Pettiford?" Mueller yelled back. "It's Tyson Mueller."

"Mueller?" A dark figure stepped out of the brush. "What the heck are you doing driving in here unannounced? I know you've got better sense than that. Somebody could have capped you as you got out."

"I couldn't call ahead. Too many ears are listening."

"Isn't that taking OPSEC a little too far?"

"No such thing now. You're not still transmitting, are you?"

"No, just listening."

"You got the message, then?"

"Not to transmit? Yeah."

"You're still not safe. They're targeting ham operators whether or not you transmit. That's why we're here."

"You had to bug out of your place?"

"Nothing left of my place. Pennsylvania is crawling with PLA," Mueller said.

"Dang!" Rory said.

"Have you encountered them here yet?"

"No. I haven't heard of them anywhere but Maryland. I've only been picking up transmissions from overseas, though, for the last week or so. The local government seized the solar panels for our repeaters for official use."

He shone a flashlight into the pickup cab.

"Come up to the house and fill me in on what's happening out there," Rory said.

After Mueller climbed back into the truck, Frank pulled through the checkpoint and followed Rory's four-wheeler for about a mile. A long gravel drive led around a large barn, a few small sheds, and finally to a large metal building. Ayden jumped down and opened Serenity's door. Finn climbed out and held Ayden's hand as they walked off behind the truck. Serenity got out, holding her abdomen, relieved not to be jostled by every bump in the road.

Until that moment, she hadn't realized how tense she'd been on the drive.

"Come on in," Rory said, approaching Mueller. The two men shook hands and then turned toward the back door of a two-story house.

Jacob unhooked Gunner's leash and the dog leaped out of the truck bed. Everyone exited the truck and followed the man down the walkway, passing more outbuildings before reaching the large two-story home. They entered through the mudroom entrance, where they left their gear but kept their weapons. The next room was a large kitchen with an oversized wood cookstove and a long center island. The light from oil lamps lit the room. It wasn't bright, but it was sufficient.

"Who are these lovely people you've brought with you?" Rory asked.

"You remember Monica," Mueller said, putting his arm around his wife's shoulders.

"And this is our daughter, Laney."

"Wow, you're all grown up," Rory said.

Laney smiled. "It happens."

Rory extended a hand to Serenity. "Nice to meet you. I'm Rory."

Mueller also introduced the rest of their group, and Rory led them into a dining room.

"Are you guys hungry? We have some rabbit left on the stove."

"No," Serenity said. Her stomach was still roiling from the curvy roads. "I'm fine, thank you."

"Anyone?" Rory asked.

"Not right now," Mueller said. "But thanks for the offer."

They all took a seat at the long, dark oak dining room table. Rory lit a collection of candles that made up the centerpiece.

Serenity watched the light dance on the walls as Rory began to describe what had transpired there since the lights went out.

"Now, about your trouble back home," he said, twirling the ends of his handlebar mustache.

Mueller informed him about what had occurred with the PLA both in Clairton and at New Eden, and then Ayden recounted everything he'd witnessed on his way to Pennsylvania.

"You sure it was the president's motorcade?" Rory asked.

"Or his designated survivor," Ayden said.

Rory frowned. "Crap! That just sucks!"

"Have you heard from California?" Serenity asked.

Rory shifted in his seat and looked down the table at where she was sitting.

"No, but a guy out in Arizona said there was heavy fighting between US and Russian forces in Los Angeles and San Francisco."

"Why would either side want those cities?" Frank asked.

"The Russians know they can't take San Diego, Camp Pendleton, or the Air Force bases. They have to stage somewhere and draw them into a fight."

"Steve—our coms guy—heard that Russia's air force took such a beating they've been flying down from Canada to avoid the coastal defenses."

"It's all just rumor and speculation until we hear from someone living there," Monica said.

Frank nodded. "True, but I'd feel better knowing we're putting some whoop-ass on those Russians and that help was coming against the Chinese soon."

"Same," Rory said. "So where are you folks headed?"

"South," Mueller said.

Serenity was confused. He'd called this man a friend, but he didn't trust him to know where they were going.

"South?"

"Mexico," Frank said. "No fighting there, we hear."

Rory looked taken aback. "You're going to Mexico? I would never have guessed that in a million years."

Mueller faked a smile. Serenity was sure Rory saw right through it.

"Yeah, Tyson Mueller is running off to Mexico."

Mueller's expression grew more serious. "Can't fight a million-man army with the folks we got left."

"I guess not. You're welcome to put down roots here—well, nearby. There are some places where folks have pulled up stakes to join family elsewhere."

"I appreciate the offer, but we're trying to stay ahead of the war," Mueller said.

"I hear ya. Offer still stands." Rory rose to his feet and pushed in his chair. "It's late. How about we all call it a night, and you guys catch a couple of hours of sleep? I'll tell you about what's happening between here and Cincinnati in the morning."

"Sounds great to me. My back hurts from riding in the back of that bouncy-ass truck," Laney said, standing and bending over to touch her toes.

"You think that was bad? Just wait until we reach Indiana. Roads suck there," Frank said.

"When we leave here, I'm driving until we get off these curvy-ass roads," Monica said.

Everyone laughed but Frank. Serenity wasn't looking forward to that part of the trip. No matter who drove, she would be carsick.

The group followed Rory down a hall off the dining room and then up a flight of stairs to an attic. Gunner bounded up the stairs and jumped onto one of the beds, wagging his tail as he waited for Finn.

"Looks like he's staked his claim," Rory said.

The attic was like another whole level, with four bedrooms down a short hall, with the bathroom in the middle.

Frank and Ayden took the room on the left, while Sadie and Jacob selected the one on the right.

"We'll take the room at the end of the hall," Mueller said, and Monica followed him there.

Serenity and Laney took the next room with the two twin beds, and Jane joined Finn in the one Gunner claimed.

"The toilet doesn't work. Sorry, ladies. You'll have to use the bucket," Rory said as he descended the steps.

"One more thing I hate about the apocalypse—that and body odor. It was something I didn't enjoy about hiking the Appalachian Trail. I couldn't adjust to not showering every day or digging a hole in the ground every time I had to go number two."

"You do eventually get used to it," Serenity said, peeling back the covers on the bed. "Showers become such a luxury that you'll treasure them when you finally get one."

Laney sat on a chair in the corner and began removing her boots. "Oh, I forgot! You used to be homeless. That had to have sucked. Did you also have to go to the bathroom outside?"

Serenity could feel the heat rise in her cheeks. She avoided discussing her time on the streets or the things she'd had to do to survive. It had been tough, but at least she'd never had to kill anyone then. "I guess we're all kind of homeless now."

"True," Laney said as she slid beneath the covers of the bed farthest from the window.

Serenity stood at the small window, letting the breeze blow in her face a moment before turning in. A coyote yipped in the distance, and Serenity tried to imagine what it was going to be like living in Wyoming, with all its open space. She'd only ever lived in towns before Jane's ranch and then the mansion. All she knew about the state was from documentaries about Yellowstone and Grand Teton National Park. Those parks were filled with bears and wolves. It would suck to escape the PLA, only to become prey to four-legged predators.

FIFTEEN

Ayden

Pettiford Farms
  Londonderry, Ohio
  Day Twenty-Four

In the light of day, Ayden got a much better look at Rory Pettiford. His white hair poked out from beneath a ball cap. He wore a light blue pullover shirt, blue work pants, and black work boots. His wife, Dianna, was five feet tall and weighed no more than one hundred and ten pounds. She was a ball of energy, though, and she had breakfast ready by the time they'd all dressed and descended the stairs after Rory called up to invite them.

On his way to the dining room, Ayden stopped and watched as Gunner chased a yellow tennis ball Finn had just thrown. The scene reminded him of his border collie, Beau, playing with Mia's boys. He wondered if the dog missed him. Would they even recognize him by the time they made it to Wyoming? His heart ached to see Mia and the boys. They seemed so far away.

When Ayden entered the dining room, children filled all twelve chairs. The youngest sat in a highchair attended by a woman in her early thirties. When Ayden's group walked in, the older boys in their family stood, picked up their plates, and sat on chairs in a nearby sunroom.

Ayden listened as the family prayed over their food. The sound of forks clanging on plates reminded him of the bunkhouse at Mia's ranch and the wranglers scarfing down food so they could get back out to the corrals to continue branding calves. It was something to see as the horse-backed wranglers roped and the branding crew branded up to three hundred head of calves and administered several vaccines to prevent diseases. It was like a well-choreographed musical symphony.

"Have a seat there, son," Rory said, directing Ayden to an open chair. A plate was set before him, and he watched Frank, Mueller, and Rory shovel food into their mouths as if it were their last meal before the gallows.

Serenity was picking at her food. She had dark circles under her eyes and looked pale.

"Serenity? You okay, sweetie?" Jane asked.

Serenity looked up but didn't answer. Instead, she leaped to her feet and bolted from the room. Sadie and Jane followed her outside through the mudroom.

"She's looking pretty pale. She's not contagious, is she?" Rory asked.

"I don't think so," Frank said. "She was injured about a week ago. Took shrapnel to the abdomen. She's still recovering."

"Might be infected," Dianna said. "We should check her temperature."

Ayden pushed back his plate and stood. "I should check on her."

Sadie and Jane were comforting her as Ayden stepped outside.

"You should lie back down and rest," Sadie said, holding Serenity's hair back from her face.

"I thought we were leaving," she said, wiping her mouth.

Finn slid in under Ayden's arm as Frank and Mueller walked up. Ayden glanced down at him and ruffled his hair.

Jane felt Serenity's forehead. "You're burning up!"

"Let's get you inside and have a look," Rory's wife said, walking up and taking Serenity's arm.

"I don't want to be any trouble," Serenity said as they headed toward the door.

"You're not. We're just going to check out your sutures. You probably ripped a stitch or two."

"She has staples," Sadie said.

"Wound dehiscence can occur with staples as well. Might need to clean up your bandage and see about a round of antibiotics."

"I was on them for the first few days," Serenity said.

"And you stopped."

"Well, my house blew up and I couldn't grab them."

"That doesn't sound like much fun," Dianna said. "Rory, have one of the boys get me my bag, and someone help me get her upstairs."

Ayden rushed over and grabbed one of Serenity's arms, while Jacob took the other.

They led her back to her bed in the attic. Ayden took a seat in the chair beside the bed. Finn crawled into his lap as Dianna entered with a pan of water and a washcloth. A tall boy about Jacob's age came in and handed Dianna a medical kit.

"Finn," Dianna said, "why don't you go with Seth and help him feed the horses?"

Finn slid from Ayden's lap and glanced up at him as if asking for approval.

"Sounds fun," Ayden said.

"But I want to stay with Serenity."

Jane walked over and took his hand. "You can come back when she's feeling better."

As Finn left with Dianna's son, Sadie and Jane gathered around the bed and watched as the woman took her temperature.

"One hundred and three." Dianna glanced over at Ayden. "You might want to step out. I'm going to have to remove her shirt to flush her wound and change her bandages."

Ayden reached over and touched Serenity's arm. "Hang in there," he said before exiting the room. He waited in the hall outside the door and listened to the conversation. After losing Clara, he wasn't ready to say goodbye to anyone else.

Serenity cursed a few times as Dianna flushed the wound.

"Hold her down," Dianna said to Sadie and Jane.

When Ayden couldn't stand to hear her in pain any longer, he returned to the dining room, where he found all of Rory's family had finished breakfast and disappeared. Jacob and Finn were playing a card game at the end of the table.

"Let me get you a new plate. I hate cold eggs," one of Rory's daughters said, picking up Ayden's nearly full plate.

"That isn't necessary," Ayden said as she disappeared into the kitchen with his food.

When she returned to the dining room, Frank, Mueller, and Rory were with her. She set the fresh plate in front of Ayden.

"Finn, do you and Jacob mind helping me?" the woman asked. "I'm going to feed the chickens and ducks." The boys stood and followed her to the kitchen.

Ayden could hear dishes clanging and quiet voices. It all seemed so normal. He wondered how other households were handling the mundane daily chores without electricity.

Rory spread a map out on the table, and everyone huddled over it.

"We're here—twelve miles east of Chillicothe," Rory said, pointing to a spot on the map.

Ayden leaned forward to see where he was pointing.

"You'll want to go south to Aberdeen, Ohio, cross the Ohio River into Kentucky, and take Highway 68 to Highway 32 right here." He circled it on the map. "It's going to add time and miles, but you want to avoid Cincinnati at all costs."

"What about roadblocks?" Frank asked. "Won't some of these small towns have them?"

"Maybe. I haven't heard of any." Rory took a drink of his coffee and then traced a route across eastern Kentucky to a small town along the river called Warsaw. Using a red pen, he marked the roads from there to Salem, Indiana. "Avoid Louisville, Kentucky. It's chaos. Cut straight across Indiana on Highway 60. That's all the information I have. After that, you're on your own."

"How do you know those roads are clear?" Mueller asked.

"Talked to a guy who took this route here from St. Louis two days ago. He said he hardly saw anyone until he got closer to Cincinnati. The roads are passable as far as stranded vehicles go. You should be able to make pretty good time."

Mueller and Frank glanced up at one another. "Sounds good to me," Frank said.

"No reports of Russian or Chinese troop movements?" Ayden asked.

"Ain't gonna lie. Some folks have reported some pretty low flyovers but no ground troops."

"What about US forces?" Mueller asked.

"Lots of planes in and out of Wright-Patterson Air Force Base in Dayton, Ohio. Heard about tons of activity down at Fort Campbell around the Kentucky/Tennessee state line—most of it so coded it was just gibberish to me."

Frank pointed to Missouri on the map. "What about Fort Leonard Wood and Whiteman Air Force Bases?"

"Oh, yeah! Whiteman—home of the B-2 Spirit stealth bombers. No, haven't heard a word about them." Rory chuckled. "Probably in stealth mode."

"And Fort Leonard Wood—they're home to the engineers," Mueller said. "Monica and I visited a buddy stationed down there a couple of years ago."

"I heard they were sent to Colorado to establish a front line against the Russians—before the Chinese landed on the East Coast."

"This is all just speculation, though," Monica said on entering the room. "Nothing more than gossip over the radio."

"Some of it comes from people reporting what they're seeing." Rory stood and pulled out a chair for her.

A knock on the door caused Ayden to jump. When Rory didn't even flinch, Ayden relaxed his shoulders and sat back. He looked across the table, and both Frank and Mueller had their hands on their holsters.

A moment later, Rory opened the door, and two small children entered and ran toward the dining table. "Poppy!" they squealed as a young woman appeared in the doorway.

"You two go outside and leave Poppy to visit with his friends," the woman said, chasing after the children.

Behind her was a heavy-set man in bib overalls.

"Hey, bro, did you guys have any trouble getting past the road-blocks?" Rory asked, reaching out to shake the man's hand.

"No. I just told the guards I was family, and they let us right through."

"Everyone, this is my brother, Calvin," Rory said, introducing the man.

Calvin described his and his family's journey there on horse-back from the adjacent county. Ayden was impressed by the little ones' riding skills but imagined it wasn't unusual for children who grew up around horses.

Ayden saw Finn and Gunner run past, followed by Calvin's son. Squeals of delight trailed off as they ran out the door.

"I'm going to go check in on Serenity and see if she needs anything." Ayden picked up his plate, then headed toward the kitchen. After leaving it beside a pail of soapy water, he ascended to the attic. Ayden knocked, and Jane said to come in. He cracked open the door and peeked inside. Serenity was on her back, with pillows elevating her feet. Looking at the deep grooves in her forehead, Ayden could tell she was in a lot of pain.

Rory's wife, Dianna, handed Serenity a glass of water and then took a pill out of a small bottle. "A broad-spectrum antibiotic," she said. "I'm going to give you two now. You've got an infection starting in your incision. This should knock it out."

Jane glanced up as Ayden entered. "The wound was oozing some. She's ripped a couple of the staples."

"We're just going to leave them open and let it drain. Even though I've flushed it, you never want to close up an infected wound."

Ayden knew even the smallest thing could become fatal without modern medical treatment. He'd seen that firsthand in his travels to third-world countries.

"Keep an eye on her. I need to go check on the boys," Sadie said.

"I wanted to speak with Dianna about getting some medical supplies if they have any to spare," Jane said.

"No worried, I'll sit with her," Ayden said. He sat in the chair beside the bed as the two women left the room.

"How are you feeling?" he asked.

"Like I've had surgery without anesthesia."

Ayden scrunched his face. "Ouch."

"Am I holding everyone up from getting back on the road?"

"No. I don't think so. Mueller and Frank were getting information from Rory about our route."

Long hours passed before Ayden heard footsteps on the stairs, and Laney entered. "Frank and my dad are loading some extra supplies donated by Rory and his family, and then they'd like to get on the road as soon as the sun goes down."

Serenity moved her legs and tried to sit up. Ayden and Laney both rushed to her side, each taking an arm to help her to her feet.

"I'm ready now. Let's go before that woman pokes my wound some more," Serenity grumbled as they led her to the door.

SIXTEEN

Mueller

Pettiford Farms
Londonderry, Ohio
Day Twenty-Four

The sun was setting as Mueller and Monica stood at the fence, watching lazy cows swat flies with their tails. Mueller turned as Ayden, Laney, and Serenity approached. Laney ran her hand along the steel pipe fence and smiled at the sight of the kid goats as they bounced on the old farm equipment and their mothers nibbled at the grass beneath it.

"We're heading out after dark," Mueller said.

Laney turned. "I'll gather Finn and Jacob."

Serenity hung her arms over a large gate and stared off at the sunset.

"Are you up to the trip, Serenity?" Mueller asked.

"I think so. I'm not one hundred percent, but I don't want to hold us up from leaving." She turned toward him. "What about you? You've been blown up twice."

Mueller touched a gash above his left eye. Every muscle in his body hurt. Like Serenity, the winding roads had made him nauseous, but he'd felt worse. He wasn't going to let it slow him down—not when so much was riding on them reaching Wyoming.

He'd passed the time since they left the bunker planning how they'd establish a home there. Once they were settled and had enough firewood and food for the long, brutal winter ahead, he planned to get out and meet folks, gather the community to resist whichever foreign military force might come against them.

"I'm fine." Mueller chuckled. "Just ready to get onto some straighter roads."

"Same!" Serenity said.

"They'd be awesome on a motorcycle," Ayden said.

"True," Frank said, approaching them. "But I'd hate all the bugs that would pelt your body."

An image of better times flashed through Mueller's mind. He and Frank were on their motorcycles, racing up Interstate 79 to Pittsburgh to attend the Steelers' football games. He imagined gone were leisure days of watching sports or riding anywhere for pleasure—at least for a good, long while.

As they stood watching Rory's farm animals, Mueller thought about how different all their lives had been since the EMP. He'd planned for a grid-down scenario for over a decade, but did any of them have a real chance with foreign troops on their soil? What would life look like in a year? Would they even survive that long?

"Let's do an inventory before we head out," Mueller said.

"Good idea. We might need to scavenge for essentials," Frank said.

Mueller, Ayden, and Frank pulled all the packs from the truck bed and began inventorying their contents. With three adults, a kid, and a dog riding in the bed, there wasn't much room for much more than the extra fuel cans. They would need to rely on what they could fit into their packs for the rest of the journey.

Ayden unzipped his pack. He had a few medical supplies, some plastic sheeting, a rope, a lighter, and little else.

"Let's get you a proper pack," Rory said. He led Ayden into the shop and then handed him a three-day tactical pack. "You can't carry enough food in that tiny bag there to sustain you during the three- or four-day trip to Mexico."

"None of us can carry enough food for three days," Serenity said. "We're already packed into the truck like a can of sardines."

"Sure you can. What do you think they feed the military every time they go out on patrols?" Rory said.

"Oh, please tell me we aren't having meals ready to eat for the entire trip," Monica said, scrunching up her nose.

"Unless you want to carry one of these heavy bags of beans with you," Rory said, gesturing to a stack of bags.

"I'd rather," Monica said.

"I just add a little Tabasco sauce to my MREs. It covers up a lot of nasty," Rory said.

"Each of you grab your three favorite MREs and quit complaining," Mueller said, opening the flaps on a box.

Serenity and Jacob took considerable time reading each label and selecting their meals.

Jacob grabbed several MREs and held them up. "These things are heavy."

"Each one weighs between a pound and a pound and a half," Frank said.

Jacob placed his bundle in Serenity's pack and she bent to lift it off the ground.

"Don't you touch that!" Mueller snapped. "You could tear your stitches again. We won't be carrying them unless something happens and we're on foot." He stuffed further MREs into his own pack.

"Let's hope that doesn't happen," she said.

"Don't worry. You can't carry your own bag, anyway. If that were to happen, I'll grab yours, and then as soon as we can, we'll distribute the stuff from your bag among us," Frank said.

Mueller made sure that each pack had sufficient survival gear so that if they found themselves on foot and separated, they'd be able to sustain themselves. Mueller lifted his own with a groan and set it on the tailgate of the truck. Bending down, he inserted his injured arm into the strap, easing it up and onto his shoulder before tackling the other strap and standing. He knew immediately that it was too heavy but refused to dump any of the items—not yet. He'd cross that bridge later if he needed to.

Once they had squared away all their gear in their packs, they joined Rory, Dianna, and their family in the driveway and said their goodbyes.

"Thanks, Rory. I owe ya, man," Frank said, slapping Rory on the back.

"Yes," Ayden said, hugging Dianna. "Thank you for your hospitality."

"You guys take care now." Dianna wrapped her arms around Jane's shoulders.

Mueller shook Rory's hand and hugged his wife, knowing he'd likely never see these people again. He'd probably never know if they survived this awful apocalypse. His circle just kept getting smaller and smaller.

After a hug from Finn and dog kisses from Gunner, Serenity climbed into the back seat of the truck. Frank shut her door and then followed Finn around to the back, assisting him and his beagle into the bed. He walked around and held the left passenger door open for Jane.

Jane stepped back. "I think I'd like to ride in the back with Finn."

"Are you sure?" Frank asked. "It's a little bumpy back there."

"Yeah. If I don't, he'll probably talk Ayden's ear off. He's taking a shine to him, I think."

Frank helped Jane into the bed of the truck and then climbed into the back seat behind Monica. He laughed as he closed the door. "Now I get to be the back seat driver."

"The hell you do. One word, and I'll—" Monica said.

"Slow down!" Frank said in a whiny, high-pitched voice. "Watch out for that pothole!"

"You better put your seat belt on, little Frankie, 'cause if you hit the back of my head flying forward, I'm going to tie you to the bumper and drag your butt all the way to there."

"Whoa!" Frank chuckled. "Vicious as ever!"

SEVENTEEN

Ayden

Pettiford Farms
Londonderry, Ohio
Day Twenty-Four

Once everyone was settled in Mueller's truck, Monica drove out of Rory's driveway and pulled back onto the county road, again taking back roads and avoiding populated areas. Finn sat next to Ayden with his beagle in his lap. As they approached the first major intersection, a roadblock came into view. Finn took Ayden's hand.

"It's okay. This is one of Rory's," Ayden said.

Finn relaxed and laid his head on Ayden's shoulder.

Mueller spoke to the guards a moment, and they waved them through. Monica steered the truck through a slalom course of barricades and proceeded south on County Road 207 through Londonderry.

Less than five minutes later, they exited the town and were back to open fields and the occasional farmhouse. When they had driven right through the second and third small towns unmolested, Ayden relaxed somewhat. No other cars were moving.

At Portsmouth Raceway in West Portsmouth, Ohio, they crossed the river into Kentucky and continued southwest, paralleling the river along a two-lane highway. Soon after they passed a little town called Tollesboro, Ayden began to notice someone had pushed cars off the road and onto the shoulder of the road, clearing both lanes of travel.

The group encountered a roadblock at the first intersection in Maysville. Frank showed them his military ID, and the officer let them pass without inspection. It seemed too good to be true.

Am I worrying for nothing?

Soon, they crossed the river again at Warsaw, Kentucky, entered Indiana, turned left, and continued west. A mile outside of Madison, Indiana, Monica increased her speed. At the next road, she took a hard right and centrifugal force pinned Ayden against the side of the truck's bed. The sharp turn had also caught Jacob and Finn off guard, and they were scrambling to right themselves.

Ayden glanced behind them and saw a truck with a light bar on its roof approaching at pace. He grabbed his rifle, watching for the pickup to make the turn with them. It didn't.

Monica made two more right turns and then took a left, and they were back on their original route. They passed a turnoff on their left just before a truck pulled in behind them. Monica floored it.

The bed of the pursuing truck emitted a series of pops, which were then followed by loud booms. A round hit the bumper of Mueller's Ford with a thud, followed by another.

"Get down!" Ayden yelled.

Ayden covered Finn with his body as Monica swerved back and forth, tossing around the occupants in the bed. When the swerving stopped, Ayden realized the gunfire had ceased as well. He sat up and looked around. No one appeared injured.

"Are you okay, Finn?" Ayden asked, sitting up.

"Squished, but okay," Finn said, pulling Gunner into his lap. "Jane?"

"I'll be fine as soon as Sadie removes her elbow from my back."

"Oh, sorry!" Sadie said, straightening.

Jacob scooted back toward Ayden and Finn. "That was some driving!"

"My mom took defensive driving lessons," Laney said.

"Guess those guys didn't." Sadie gestured to the truck that had pursued them, which now lay sideways in a ditch, smoke billowing from its hood.

"That's good to know," Jane said. "I thought for a moment we were going to end up there ourselves."

"I'm shocked none of those bullets struck us," Sadie said.

"We're blessed," Jane said.

"Very." Sadie closed her eyes and exhaled.

Monica didn't slow down. They tore into the tiny village of Blocher, Indiana, where she made another sharp left turn and raced west along Highway 56, finally stopping before the bridge across Pigeon Roost Creek.

Frank and Mueller exited the vehicle cab, flicking on a flashlight. "We got lucky there, boys," Frank said, making his way to the back.

"Why have we stopped?" Laney asked.

"We're running on fumes. Time to fuel up." Mueller dropped the tailgate and grabbed one of the four fuel cans. He lifted it into the air with ease.

"That's not good," Ayden said.

"What happened to the gasoline in it?" Sadie asked.

Frank shone his flashlight's beam on the can, illuminating the bullet-sized hole through one side and out the other. He inspected the inside of the bed of the truck, poking a finger into the hole through the metal. Frank lifted another fuel jug, shook it, and gasoline poured from its side as well. "Damn, the bullet went through all four cans!"

"How much fuel do you think is left in them?" Laney asked.

"Maybe ten gallons."

"That won't take us far."

"One hundred and twenty miles, depending on how fast we drive," Finn said.

"How do you know that?" Jacob asked.

"Rory said the truck gets twelve miles per gallon."

"Where will one hundred and twenty miles get us to?" Sadie asked.

"Vincennes." Monica exited the truck with the map in her hands. "Vincennes, Indiana. We should look for more fuel cans and gasoline along the way."

Frank filled the tank with what they had left and tossed the damaged cans into the ditch.

Monica gave him a disapproving look.

"You want to carry them with us until we find a dumpster to put them in?" Frank asked in a sarcastic tone.

Monica shrugged and returned to the driver's seat.

Ayden, Finn, and Gunner settled back against the truck cab next to Jane as Monica put the truck into gear and accelerated west.

The roads leading into Salem, Indiana, had also been cleared of vehicles. Monica slowed to a stop on the outskirts. Ayden rapped on the cab's back window, and Frank pushed it open.

"What's up?"

"Roadblock ahead," Frank said. "We're checking the map for a way around it." After a brief pause, he said, "There's a bypass around the town."

"They'll likely have others posted along that," Mueller said. "If we take this crossroad, we can reconnect with Highway 56 on the west side of town."

"That's a lot more miles. Do we have the fuel for that?"

"It's better than risking having the truck taken from us at a checkpoint—or worse."

Monica reversed the pickup and turned down the rural road. They had to zigzag through the outskirts to avoid a few checkpoints but didn't encounter any resistance. Thirty minutes later, she slowed the Ford and pulled over onto the shoulder. She put the truck into Park. Ayden climbed over the side of the truck's bed and stood next to Mueller's door. Moonlight glinted off a monocular he pulled from his pack.

"What are you looking for?" Ayden asked as Mueller scanned the area ahead of them.

"Movement. Any signs of people on the roadway. Monica thought she saw people crossing on foot ahead. I don't want to drive into an ambush."

"Ambush?" Serenity asked from the back seat.

Ayden rubbed his stubbled chin. They were still more than twelve hundred miles from Mia's ranch in Farson, Wyoming. Twelve hundred more miles of white-knuckling every mile, watching out for trouble.

"There appear to be people camping at the gas station stop ahead," Mueller said, not removing the monocular from his eye.

Ayden glanced in that direction but saw nothing.

Mueller lowered the monocular and reached over to retrieve his rifle. "Better tell the folks in the back to get ready."

"Isn't there another way around to avoid them?" Serenity asked.

"That's our turn there." Monica nodded to the intersection. "We don't have the fuel to backtrack for miles and find an alternate route."

Frank handed Serenity her rifle. She clutched the AR-15 tight between her legs with the butt on the floorboard.

"You might want to hold that in your lap so you can be ready for a shootout."

Serenity gripped the rifle in her lap with the barrel resting on the window opening.

Ayden climbed back into the bed of the truck, grabbed his rifle, and faced the front. "Everyone get down. We're in for a bumpy ride."

Monica drove slowly past a fast-food restaurant. Ahead, burning trash cans illuminated a gas station parking lot filled with rows of makeshift tents fashioned out of tarps, small blankets, and anything else people could use to shield themselves from the sun. As they approached, a man stood and faced the Ford. Someone else peeked out from behind a blue tarp.

"Get down, Laney," Ayden yelled as Monica sped up.

EIGHTEEN

Mueller

Highway 60
Mitchell, Indiana
Day Twenty-Four

As Monica floored the accelerator, the Ford's headlights slashed through the darkness, illuminating two men and a woman who darted into the road, waving their arms frantically to flag them down. Mueller, adrenaline coursing through his veins, swung the rifle up to his shoulder, his left arm burning as he sighted down the barrel at the figures now frozen in the beams of light.

"Tyson?" Monica's voice held a note of panic.

"Frank, keep your sights on the man in the ball cap," Mueller said calmly.

Leaning out the window, Mueller trained his rifle on the man, the ball cap centered in his crosshairs.

"Tyson!" Monica repeated, her tone more urgent this time.

As the vehicle decelerated, three more figures stepped onto the road. Mueller's eyes darted between the newcomers, searching for any sign of a threat. His focus narrowed as one man reached behind his back—too smooth, too practiced a motion to be inno-cent. Without hesitation, Mueller squeezed the trigger, the report of the rifle echoing. The man collapsed, a stark, still form on the asphalt as the truck sped past.

Monica took the turn onto Highway 60 a bit too sharply in her haste, almost sending the truck careening off the road. Mueller ducked back inside and rolled up the window just as the vehicle steadied. The engine whined under the strain as they barreled down the highway toward Shoals, Indiana.

About five miles down the road, Monica's grip faltered, and she slowed the truck, pulling over onto the shoulder with a gravelly crunch. Before they had come to a complete stop, she flung the door open and vomited. She staggered out and leaned heavily over the guardrail.

Mueller stepped out and approached her, concern etching his features. "Are you okay?"

"That scared the bejesus out of me. My hands are shaking so bad, I don't think I can drive." Her voice trembled.

"Let Frank take the wheel then." Mueller gently guided her back toward the truck.

Monica nodded and shuffled over to Frank's door. "I think you should drive for a while," she said softly. She climbed into the back seat as Frank assumed his position behind the wheel.

They continued their journey, soon approaching a bridge over the East Fork White River in the small town of Shoals, Indiana. "We need to find fuel, pronto," Frank said, eyeing the fuel gauge, which hovered near empty.

"Take that left there, and let's find our replacement fuel cans. Maybe we'll get lucky and find a car that can siphon enough to get us to Mount Vernon, Illinois," Frank said.

Monica leaned forward, resting her hand on Mueller's seat. "Are you planning on stopping in on Billie?" she asked, her tone laced with suspicion.

"I thought we might." Mueller avoided her gaze. He knew she

wouldn't appreciate visiting his ex-wife, Billie Jean. The history between them was complicated, made more so since Billie's new husband had been married to Monica's best friend before the affair.

"Why?" Monica pressed.

"I left something there," Frank interjected before Mueller could respond. "When I stopped by to visit with Billie's husband, I had him hold on to a weapon or two for me. I'd like to retrieve them on our way."

Monica tapped Mueller on the shoulder. "If that witch says one word to me—"

"We won't even get out of the truck, dear," Mueller assured her quickly, hoping to ease her concerns.

Upon crossing over the railroad tracks, the truck's headlights swept across the scattered vehicles.

"Looks like a salvage yard," Frank said.

Mueller's eyebrows rose. "Worth checking out."

Frank shut off the headlights, pulled into the auto salvage yard lot, and parked between two rusty old trucks. Moonlight glinted off an ancient Dodge truck's large side mirror.

As Mueller moved to exit the truck, Monica's hand rested on his shoulder, stopping him.

"Where do you think you're going?" she snapped.

"To help Frank find a fuel can and maybe some fuel to siphon," Mueller replied, his tone firm.

"I got this, Ty. Take it easy," Frank said, easing open his door. "I'll take Ayden with me this time."

"I'm fine. You two need to stop treating me like I'm disabled or something," Mueller said, his frustration clear.

"Are you going to tell me you didn't suffer a concussion either time you were blown up?"

"I—" Mueller stammered.

Monica cut him off. "That's a lie. You know you did. Just sit right there. I'll go with Frank."

Ayden appeared next to Mueller's window. "I got this, Ms. Monica."

"See?" Monica said, a hint of relief in her voice. "He wants to go."

Mueller studied him. The city boy didn't even know how to hold his weapon right. "Frank?" Mueller expected Frank to back him up.

"Fine by me," Frank said, easing his door closed.

"Okay," Mueller conceded reluctantly. He turned to Ayden, his gaze serious. "Watch your sound and light discipline. You'll want to get in and out without detection."

"Sure thing," Ayden replied, shouldering his rifle.

Whatever that means.

"Keep your barrel pointed at the ground and your finger off the trigger."

Giving him a thumbs-up, Ayden fell in behind Frank, and the two disappeared into the darkness.

Mueller sat back heavily in the passenger seat, his body aching as Monica's words about his concussion echoed in his ears, stirring a flood of memories he had been pushing to the back of his mind. He closed his eyes, leaned his head against the cool glass of the window, and let the memories wash over him.

The battle in Clairton with the PLA had been one of the most harrowing experiences of his life. He remembered the tension in the air that day, thick with the smell of sweat and fear. The PLA forces had been relentless in their attack, and Keith had taken cover in an abandoned house after being injured by a PLA bullet. Mueller, after he and Amos set off the fireworks as a distraction, had sprinted up the street toward the abandoned house where Serenity had left her father. When Mueller spotted the PLA soldiers closing in, he raced up the walkway and pulled Keith from the home seconds before their world erupted into noise and fire. An explosion, so sudden and so close, had torn through the frail structure of the building. Mueller remembered the deafening roar, the blast of heat, and then a suffocating blackness as the house collapsed on top of them, burying them in burning debris.

Time lost meaning under the rubble. Mueller couldn't tell how long he lay unconscious, the weight of the destroyed home pressing down on him, the heat searing his skin. When consciousness crept back, it brought with it a sharp, agonizing pain and the acrid smell of smoke and charred wood.

With a groan, Mueller had started to move, pushing aside chunks of wood and plaster, his hands shaking, his every breath a fiery agony. He found Keith nearby, semiconscious and disoriented. Gathering every ounce of strength he had left, Mueller had thrown the debris off them and hoisted Keith up, practically dragging him one-handed through the streets of Clairton. Keith had been a dead weight, his injuries severe, unconscious due to shock and pain.

They had stumbled through the devastated streets, dodging sporadic gunfire and falling debris. Every step was a battle against the overwhelming urge to collapse and surrender to the darkness that edged his vision. But Mueller kept moving, driven by a single-minded determination not to let Keith—or himself—die in that godforsaken place.

They had reached the railroad tracks on the west side of town, an open, vulnerable stretch of land that seemed an eternity away from the relative safety of New Eden. There on the tracks, Ayden had found them, barely conscious and covered in ash and blood.

Monica's voice brought him back to the present, her hand warm on his shoulder. "Tyson, are you with us?"

Mueller opened his eyes, meeting her concerned gaze. "Yeah, I'm here," he muttered, the images of Clairton still vivid behind his eyes.

"We need you whole and healthy." Monica gave his shoulder a gentle squeeze. "Rest now. We can handle things for a bit."

Mueller nodded, leaning back in his seat, the physical and

emotional scars of that day in Clairton etched deep. He'd lost so many friends that day—all good people and so many more in the PLA's attack on New Eden. Mueller knew despite Monica's wishes, he didn't have time to rest or heal because the road ahead would eventually require everyone to work together to make it through.

NINETEEN

Ayden

Shoals Auto Salvage
Shoals, Indiana
Day Twenty-Four

As the darkness enveloped them, Ayden followed Frank along a chain-link fence that rattled in the night breeze. The moon, just a sliver in the sky, cast only enough light to deepen the shadows around them, turning every corner into a potential hiding spot. Their path led to the back of a large metal shop building, where the air smelled faintly of old rubber and motor oil—a scent that reminded Ayden of late nights helping his best friend, Reid McFarland, work on his jeep back in Wyoming.

Ayden momentarily wondered whether he'd ever see Reid again, who lived in an apartment in Lander, Wyoming. His refrigerator was always bare. How would he find food or fresh water? He didn't hunt or fish. Would he have the forethought to set out on foot for Mia's? *Maybe*, Ayden thought. As they rounded the corner of the building, he comforted himself with the image of Reid hanging out with the wranglers at Mia's ranch. He chuckled to himself at the thought of his friend riding a horse for the first time.

Frank led the group around to the south side of the building, using his flashlight sparingly. He flicked it on briefly, then off, guiding them with deliberate movements as if he knew exactly where to find a fuel can.

"Frank, you look like you know a lot about… well, everything survival-related. Were you in the military?" Ayden whispered.

"Yeah, I was. Did two tours in the Middle East before moving into a training role back home."

"You ever consider joining in the fight against the PLA?" Ayden asked.

"When the attacks began, I had my family to worry about. Now, I need to get the Muellers to safety. But once they're secure, I plan to join back up. Those commies are going to pay for taking my family from me."

"I want to fight back," Ayden said, his voice cracking. "They took my sister from me."

"You will—you have been, from what I've heard. You're learning, and when the time's right, we'll take the fight to them."

When they reached the bay doors, Frank paused and flashed the light from his rifle's scope through a small, grimy window in the door. The beam briefly illuminated a cluttered interior, filled with stacks of disused parts and tools.

"See anything?" Ayden murmured, his voice barely rising above the soft howling of the wind.

"Maybe," Frank murmured, moving to the next door to repeat the motion. He paused, the light steady. "There! Under the bench." He nodded toward a red fuel can just visible behind a rolling cart.

As Frank reached down to roll up the door, a loud squeak shattered the relative silence of the night, causing both men to freeze. "Crap!" Frank hissed under his breath.

Ayden pointed to a smaller, man-sized door. "I'll try that one," he said.

"I'll watch your six," Frank said, his tone serious as Ayden moved toward the door.

Testing the knob, Ayden found it locked. He examined the door —it was flimsy, the wood soft and weathered, not the fortified steel he had expected of a business. It felt insubstantial, like it belonged in an old rural home rather than a shop. "I think I can pop it open pretty quick," he murmured back to Frank.

"Remember, we need it quiet."

"I don't think it will make much noise. It's not very solid."

"Okay, dude. Give it a try, but be ready to respond if some old boy flies out of one of those houses there."

"Roger that," Ayden said, a slight smile flickering on his lips as he adopted Frank and Mueller's military lingo. Positioning himself, he turned his back to the door and delivered a swift backward kick. The door popped open with a dull thud, more a sigh than a bang.

"Good job," Frank murmured, stepping past him to enter. "Stay here and stand watch while I have a look around."

"I thought we were just here for the fuel can?" Ayden peered into the shadow-filled interior of the shop.

"I'd like to gather some tools in case we need to work on that old rust bucket later," Frank explained, his voice fading as he moved deeper into the shop.

"Don't let Mueller hear you call it that. I think he's kind of fond of her," Ayden quipped.

Frank chuckled, his silhouette disappearing from view.

Left alone, Ayden stood guard at the doorway, the night sounds now more pronounced. The distant hoot of an owl, the rustling of small creatures in the underbrush, and the occasional creak of the shop settling all created a backdrop of eerie normalcy.

Then, a sudden crack—a branch snapping underfoot somewhere in the darkness—sent a chill down Ayden's spine. His hand tightened around his rifle as he scanned the darkness, every sense heightened.

A moment later, Frank reemerged. "Here, grab these," he whispered, handing Ayden several heavy-duty flashlights, a box of batteries, and several rolls of duct tape.

Ayden stuffed them into his pack as Frank disappeared back inside the shop.

Another branch snapped, and Ayden moved back, crouching in the dark doorway.

The sharp silhouette of an older man emerged from the shadows, a shotgun cradled in his arms.

Heart pounding, Ayden stepped deeper into the shop and eased the door shut just as the man's voice cut through the silence, rough and suspicious.

"Who's there?"

Without hesitating, Ayden turned and darted through the dark building, his voice barely a whisper as urgency propelled him. "Frank!" he hissed. "Someone's outside. We have to go!"

He found Frank exiting an office, the glow of a flashlight briefly illuminating his calm face. His rifle dangled on its single point sling, and Frank held two sodas in his hands. "Are you sure?"

"Yes! He's got a shotgun. Let's go, man! I don't want to shoot some old man," Ayden said in a panic.

Frank shoved the drinks into Ayden's hands, then whirled around and disappeared back into the shadows.

"Come on, Frank! We have to go!" Ayden called after him.

"Not without the fuel can."

Moments later, Frank reappeared, a tool bag in one hand and the red fuel can in the other. "Give me the sodas. I'll put them in the bag with the tools."

Ayden handed over the drinks, and Frank stuffed them into the bag. Then Frank handed the heavy tool bag and the fuel can back to Ayden. "You're going to run to the truck. I'll watch your back."

"If I get shot in the ass with buckshot, I'm not going to be happy," Ayden grumbled.

Frank chuckled as he unlocked the front door and yanked it open.

Ayden didn't need another prompt. He sprinted across the parking lot, the cool night breeze refreshing on his sweaty face. Reaching the truck, Ayden tossed the bag and the can into the bed and vaulted over the tailgate, landing hard on something solid—Jacob's boot.

"Ouch!" Jacob cried out.

"Sorry!" Ayden said, managing to sit up.

As Frank made his dash toward the truck, the old man rounded the back of the shop, cursing. "You thieves! I'm gonna teach you to steal from me!"

Flickers of light from flashlight beams suddenly appeared from buildings on their right.

The truck's engine roared to life, and then the driver's door swung open just as Frank neared. An instant later, Frank jumped in behind the wheel, and the truck lurched forward, gravel flying as the engine howled.

Just then, the loud boom of the shotgun tore through the night.

Ayden tensed, waiting for the sound of pellets hitting the truck. His body braced for impact. But all he heard were the truck's tires crunching gravel and the old man's fading curses. Relief washed over him as it became clear they had escaped unscathed, the danger momentarily behind them. Yet the night's events left a lingering unease as they sped away into the darkness. Scavenging for supplies was nearly as dangerous as moving through PLA-held territory. How bad would it have sucked to get shot over two soft drinks, some tools, and an empty fuel can?

As Frank sped west through town, Ayden braced himself for the next stop, knowing next time would be even more dangerous, as they'd be stealing gasoline.

TWENTY

Serenity

Shoals Auto Salvage
Shoals, Indiana
Day Twenty-Four

"Turn right!" Mueller yelled over the sound of the second boom. "Turn right! Now!"

Serenity held on to the back of Mueller's seat as Frank took the sharp turn at the next street. Just as suddenly, the road curved to the left, and Frank floored it, racing to the next avenue.

"Here! Here! Here! Take the right!" Mueller said, his voice rising over the roar of the engine.

"Get us the hell out of here, Frank!" Monica yelled as lights began lighting up in the windows of the homes they passed.

Frank yanked the wheel hard to the right, and the tires bounced over railroad tracks as they sped north.

"Left! Left!" Mueller barked.

The old Ford jostled violently as Frank, barely lifting his foot from the accelerator, clipped the curb while turning onto Highway 150. The truck tilted to the left before righting itself with a thud that sent a shudder through its frame and sent waves of fresh pain through Serenity.

She risked a glance back through the rear window, squinting into the darkness to check on those in the truck bed, but the poor visibility prevented her from discerning any details.

As they raced westward, Serenity slid open the back window. "Is everyone okay back there?" she shouted against the wind whipping through the opening.

Ayden began counting heads. "One. Two. Three…" His voice paused momentarily. "Finn?"

"I'm okay," Finn called back, his voice slightly muffled by the rush of air.

"We're good," Ayden said.

Monica twisted around in her seat. "Laney?" she called with concern in her voice.

"I'm good, Mom."

"Keep a close watch for headlights approaching. They might decide to come after us," Monica said.

"I'm on it," Laney said.

Monica closed the window and smoothed back her hair as she turned to face the front.

A few miles down the road, Frank slowed.

"What are you doing?" Serenity called. "Why are you slowing down?"

Without answering her question, Frank pointed toward a grouping of several metal buildings surrounded by a chain-link fence on the right-hand side of the road. "What do you think, Ty?"

Mueller glanced to his left. "There's nothing else around. Might be able to get in and out without detection. There's a couple of trucks parked in a row in front of that second building."

"What are we doing?" Serenity's voice pitched with panic. "We just about got shot less than five minutes ago, and you want to stop again?"

"No choice," Frank said. "We're running on fumes. We have to find fuel, or we're walking from here."

Serenity twisted in her seat, eyes wide as she scanned the horizon for any sign of pursuit.

Frank pulled the truck to a stop at the gate and cut off the headlights.

In seconds, Ayden appeared at the driver's door with the fuel can in his hand. "We don't have a siphoning hose," he said. "How are we going to fill this?"

"We don't need a hose. You can't siphon fuel from these new model trucks, anyway."

"How are we going to get the fuel out of the tank and into the can, then?" Ayden asked as Frank exited the Ford.

"You're going to climb under one and poke a hole in the fuel tank."

"Okay," Ayden said, but it sounded more like a question.

Serenity leaned forward, eager to hear how they were going to accomplish this mission.

"You see that building with the huge overhead doors, Ayden?" Frank said.

"Yeah."

"They work on county vehicles in there, which means they chain the oil and other fuels. They drain it into pans."

"Oh!" Ayden said, drawing out the word.

Laney appeared just as Mueller opened his truck door and stuck one leg out.

Serenity rolled down her window.

"I'll sprint around the curve in the road and watch for head-lights," Laney said.

An instant later, Jane appeared, her rifle shouldered. "I'll walk the other way and make sure no one is coming from that direction."

Serenity started to exit the truck, but Monica grabbed her arm. "Stay put. If we need to leave in a hurry, you'll just slow us down."

Serenity sat back, frustrated that she was a burden and not a help. She chewed her bottom lip, cursing the PLA under her breath for putting her in this weakened condition.

Monica stepped out and joined Mueller as they waited for Frank and Ayden to return with the gasoline to refuel the truck.

While the minutes ticked by there in the dark, Serenity opened the back glass and listened to Finn's conversation with her mother, Sadie. His voice brimmed with the excitement and curiosity of a precocious six-year-old who had absorbed volumes of information before the world changed.

"Sadie, did you know the Grand Tetons are some of the youngest mountains in North America? They're really high and steep because they're not worn down by weather like older mountains," Finn explained in a rush. "They rise straight up seven thousand feet from the valley! That's like stacking seven thousand rulers on top of each other!"

He paused, and Serenity pictured the towering, snow-capped peaks.

"And there's this valley called Jackson Hole right by the mountains. It's famous for skiing. I read about the aerial tram that goes up to the top of Rendezvous Mountain. It used to take people up so they could ski down. It's really long, over ten thousand feet or something."

Finn drew in a quick breath before sighing heavily. His tone shifted from enthusiasm to contemplative, almost as if he were solving a puzzle in his head, imagining the expedition they might undertake together in a changed world. "I wonder how someone might climb up that mountain now to ski down. It must be a big adventure to walk all the way up. Maybe we could find a path or follow where the tram used to go. It could be like a real expedition, right, Sadie?"

"Sure, Finn." Sadie sounded distracted, but Finn didn't seem to notice.

"I'll climb it with you," Jacob said. "Wouldn't it be cool to tube down it?"

"Yeah!" Finn said.

"Remember, Mom? Remember when you and Dad used to take Renny and me to Sled Hill back home?"

Serenity's mother didn't respond. She likely didn't remember. She'd always waited in the car, too drunk and high to walk on the snow. Jacob grew quiet, probably recalling the same scenario. Sadie hadn't been that kind of mother.

"I wonder what moose tastes like," Finn said, changing the subject.

Before Jacob or Sadie could respond, Frank and Ayden reappeared, each carrying two fuel cans.

TWENTY-ONE

Ayden

Martin County Maintenance Facility
Shoals, Indiana
Day Twenty-Five

With the Ford's fuel tank filled and everyone back inside the vehicle, Frank pulled back onto the highway and continued west. Ayden, with Finn and his dog, Gunner, back at his side, leaned his head back against the cab and closed his eyes. By the time they were skirting Vincennes, Indiana, an hour later, the adrenaline that had flooded his body during the two stops in Shoals was declining. It left him now feeling weak and depleted.

Ayden was no stranger to adrenaline rushes. Before this chaos, he had been an adrenaline junkie, constantly pushing the limits with bigger and riskier challenges. Yet none of those past thrills could compare to the relentless, uncontrollable danger of their current reality. In his extreme sports adventures, there had always been some element of control. Now, he felt at the mercy of circumstances beyond his control. He pondered the cruel randomness of survival—why had he lived while his sister had not? Why had Tina opened those closet doors only to meet her end? These thoughts haunted him, along with the faces of those he'd lost in the past weeks.

His thoughts drifted to Mia and the boys. He was terrified at the prospect of witnessing their potential fate, akin to that of Tina, Lunch Box, and the others. The thought was unbearable, and he knew if he dwelled on it, it could very well break him.

Finn, perhaps sensing the heavy mood, snuggled closer to Ayden and rested his head against his shoulder. Ayden responded by wrapping an arm around the boy, feeling Finn's tension dissipate. Gunner, ever the loyal companion, laid his head on Finn's knee, adding to the small comfort they found in each other. Ayden's heart ached with the weight of his responsibility and his inability to guarantee absolute safety for anyone, echoing his helplessness in protecting his sister.

Despair loomed, threatening to drag him into a deep, dark abyss, a place from which he feared he might never emerge. But then, something within him shifted—anger, fierce and burning, began to simmer in his gut. He was tired of running and exhausted from being a pawn in the PLA's cruel game. His fists clenched, and his jaw tightened as he imagined standing defiant in the streets, confronting the enemy head on. Frank's plan resonated with him now more than ever: ensure the group's safety in Wyoming, then turn and face their aggressors and fight back with everything he had. This urge to stand and fight, to protect what was left and to reclaim their freedom, coursed through him, replacing the despair.

As Frank steered the old Ford into the tiny town of Parkersburg, Illinois, Ayden sat up on high alert. He grabbed his rifle and moved more to the center of the bed, ready to take on any threat that might come at them.

Laney did the same, climbing over Jacob and kneeling close to the tailgate. "It almost seems deserted," she said as they drove through unmolested.

"It has to be nearing five a.m. The sun is just cresting," Ayden said, gesturing to the faint light in the eastern sky.

"I hope we make it to Mount Vernon before daybreak," Laney said. "I don't want people taking potshots at us from their homes or something."

An hour later, the sky was light with early morning light as Frank steered the truck off the highway and headed north along a county road. Moments later, they stopped at a gravel drive flanked by two single-story homes. The front door of the home on the left opened, and a beautiful woman in her forties stepped out, pulling her pink satin robe tight against her nearly perfect female form.

Frank cranked down his window. "Hi there, Billie Jean!"

"Frank Sonderborg? What the hell are you doing here?"

Monica rolled down her window.

Billie Jean's hand went up. "Monica," she said flatly. "Hey, Laney," the woman said, glancing into the bed of the truck.

"I just stopped by to pick up something I left with Barrett. We won't stay but a minute."

"Barrett isn't here. He never came home from San Antonio."

"Texas? What was he doing down there?" Frank asked.

Billie Jean shrugged. "Work of some kind. You know Barrett. Always has something going. What is he holding for you?"

Frank opened his door and stepped out. He glanced back at Monica as he crossed Billie Jean's front lawn.

"I hope he hurries before my mom gets set off," Laney said in a hushed tone.

"Why?" Finn asked. "Doesn't she like her?" He shifted, hanging his arms over the side of the truck's bed. "I think she's pretty," he whispered.

"It's a long story," Laney said, glancing at the truck cab.

Ayden followed her gaze. While Monica glared at the woman, Mueller's head was turned in the opposite direction, staring out at the expansive field of corn, its brown leaves blowing in the early morning wind.

Mueller's door opened, and he stepped out.

"Where do you think you're going, Tyson Luke Mueller?" Monica spat.

Without stopping, Mueller crossed the roadway and the ditch that ran alongside it, stopping next to the stalks of corn. He parted the leaves and disappeared into the field.

Ayden's gaze shifted back to Frank and Billie Jean as they entered her house. As they did, Laney stood and climbed over the tailgate. "Keep an eye on my mom. I'm going to help my dad pick corn."

"Me too!" Jacob said, jumping down.

"I want to help!" Finn said, rushing to the tailgate.

Ayden climbed over, lowered it, and helped him down. Gunner started to follow. "No, boy. You stay here. We don't have time to wait around while you chase rabbits."

Monica's door opened. "What the heck, people? We're leaving soon."

"Corn!" Jacob said, pointing to the field as he ran toward it.

"It's just nasty field corn. It's dried-out, and the kernels are hard. You can't eat that. It's for animals."

Sadie sat on the tailgate, swinging her feet as Ayden walked to the edge of the road.

"You can make cornmeal with it," a sultry voice said behind him.

Ayden spun around to find Billie Jean and Frank approaching. Monica stood next to the truck with her hands balled into fists.

"It's about all I've lived on for the last two weeks," Billie Jean said.

"Well, it looks like you could afford to miss a meal or two," Monica bit back.

Frank stepped between them. In his hands, he carried a large Pelican case. "Um... she—" Frank started to say.

Monica cut him off. "No! Absolutely not!"

"She just needs—"

"She needs my boot up her—"

Mueller's voice cut through the air. "Monica!"

She whirled around. "Tyson Mueller. If you dare—"

"Ty, she just needs a ride over to Macon, Missouri. It's on our way," Frank interjected.

"She can walk her butt there. She needs the exercise to lose some of that fat." Monica shook her fist as she attempted to step around Frank.

Frank extended his arm, blocking her.

Billie Jean smiled smugly. She dropped her hands to her sides and poked out her chest. She glared back at Monica but said nothing.

"Billie can ride in the back. Means you don't have to look at her," Frank said.

"But I'd smell her nasty—" Monica stopped mid-sentence and glanced back as Finn walked up.

"I can pay you. You like money—as I recall," Billie Jean said. "Isn't that how you got Ty?"

As Monica leaped forward, Frank caught her by the shirt. It ripped from his hand, and Monica fell flat at Billie Jean's feet. Flushing, Monica quickly got to her knees.

"Yeah! That's the position."

"Stop! Both of you," Mueller said.

Laney rushed to her mother's side.

"Billie, grab your stuff, and let's get going!"

"Oh, hell no!" Monica said, scrambling to her feet.

Laney grabbed her before she got too far.

"Mom!"

Monica spun around and stomped back to the truck. "Fine! I'll be in the cab."

"I'll wait with you," Sadie said, climbing into the back seat next to Serenity.

"You should pull the truck into the garage out of view—unless you want the Costantini boys to steal it like they've taken everything else around here," Billie Jean said.

"Too bad they didn't carry you off. I guess they don't like their women old and trashy."

"I guess you're safe then," Billie Jean said.

"Will you two stop it? You're upsetting the kids," Mueller said.

Ayden glanced back. Finn and Jacob were snickering, appearing to enjoy the show.

Mueller stepped between them and took his wife's hand. "Just hurry up, Billie. I'd like to cross over into Missouri before noon."

"There are fuel cans in the garage and a thirty-five fuel caddy to fill them with gas. Should be enough to get me to Macon."

"I'll grab those," Frank said, placing his case in the back of the truck.

"What's in the case?" Laney asked.

"Want to see?"

She smiled and nodded.

He placed it on the tailgate and opened it.

"Where on earth did you get that?" she asked, her eyes widening.

Ayden stepped up beside her. "What is it?"

A huge grin spread across Frank's face. "A STEYR ARMS GL 40 grenade launcher!"

"That would blow some stuff up!" Laney said.

"Are the Chinese in Missouri, too?" Finn asked.

Mueller turned to face him. "No, not that I've heard. But we need to be ready for anything, right?"

Finn nodded. "But I don't have a weapon."

As Frank and Jacob set off to grab the fuel cans, Mueller pulled a small can of pepper spray from a pouch on his tactical belt. "Is this okay?" he asked, directing his question to Jane, who was standing beside Finn.

"Only for emergencies. Otherwise, you keep that in your pocket. It's not a toy."

"I know, Grammy Jane. Mommy had some. She kept it on her bedside table. She sprayed Daddy in the face with it one time. He got very, very mad." Finn's expression fell.

Jane took the pepper spray from Mueller. She bent to her grandson's level. "This is how you use it." She held it out and pointed at the roadside ditch. "Flick the top and press down on this. I'm not going to do it now, but you get the idea."

"Okay, Grammy. I've got it. I'll keep it clipped on my belt until I have to use it on one of those commie bas—"

"Finn Conner McKeown!" Jane barked.

Finn chuckled as Gunner ran circles around him. "Sorry!"

"Right, everyone. Let's load back up and be ready to roll when Billie gets back," Mueller said.

Monica took his hand. "I'll drive."

"Maybe Ayden or I should drive. You and Frank have been up all night," Laney said.

Ayden stepped forward. "Yeah, I could drive. You guys could get some rest."

Mueller put his arm around Monica's shoulders. "I agree, sweetness. The young'uns have this one."

"If you lie down in the back, the wind isn't too bad, Mom," Laney said.

"I'm not sleeping next to that skank," Monica said.

"You need to, Monica. We have a long way to go."

"I'll sleep after we drop that man-stealing hoe off in Macon," Monica said.

Laney leaned in close to her mother. "You can't really *steal* a person, Mom."

"Oh, really?" Monica stomped off and climbed into the back seat of the truck.

Ayden leaned against the driver's door, waiting for everyone to get in. It was dead quiet. For a moment, he could imagine how dull life must have been living there before the EMP. After leaving New York City, Ayden hadn't remained in one place long enough to get bored—not before his car accident and meeting Mia. He'd once feared boredom more than anything in life—now, he longed for it. The thought he might never again visit places like Nepal and Zambezi River or enjoy the view from the summit of El Capitan saddened Ayden. A fresh wave of rage gripped him, knowing that a long battle and great hardship lay ahead and life would never return to "normal." Somehow, he'd have to learn to adjust or let the rage that had ignited in him burn until it consumed him.

TWENTY-TWO

Ayden

Billie Jean Whiteside's Residence
Mount Vernon, Illinois
Day Twenty-Five

Less than two hours after Billie Jean returned to the truck with her suitcase, climbing into the back with Sadie, Jane, Frank, Gunner, and the two boys, Ayden steered the old Ford around the tiny village of Pocahontas before turning it toward Staunton, Illinois, and avoiding the most populated areas of the greater St. Louis, Missouri, region, which over two million called home.

By noon, they had crossed over the Illinois River at Hardin. Ayden held his breath all the way across, anxious about what might await them on the opposite side. When they neared the center, and Ayden could see that no ambush awaited them, he let out a heavy sigh of relief.

"I'm surprised, too," Mueller said. "I expected the bridges to be rubble or guarded like those back over the Monongahela River back home."

"We haven't seen any evidence of PLA or US troops since we

left Pennsylvania. Maybe they stopped their advance," Laney said from her seat between Ayden and her father.

Ayden glanced into the rearview mirror. Both Monica and Serenity had their eyes closed. He hoped they were getting some much-needed sleep, but he doubted it. Even though he'd shut his eyes when he was in the truck bed, he was unable to relax fully, fearing an attack at any moment. PLA drones were silent, flying thousands of miles above their intended targets.

"It may be months before the fighting reaches the Midwest," Mueller said. "But, eventually, the US forces will become low on bullets, bombs, and personnel. Citizens will be the only thing standing between the PLA and the fertile croplands of this region."

"What about the Russians?" Laney asked.

"I doubt they'll make it past the Rocky Mountains. If they somehow get control of the military on the West Coast, winter snows will likely hold them up at the higher elevations soon. That would give our military time for allies to resupply them, maybe join the fight."

"Shouldn't we have seen allies by now?" Ayden asked.

"Not if what we heard was true—that cyberattacks and EMPs struck them as well," Mueller said.

Ayden turned north and paralleled the river, keeping a keen eye out for any military forces. Soon, they entered Kampsville, Illinois, and turned west again, away from the Illinois River and heading toward the Mississippi River. Ayden slowed as they approached the Champ Clark Bridge spanning the mighty Mississippi, crossed into Missouri, and entered the city of Louisiana.

Immediately, Ayden stomped on the gas and raced west along Highway 54, eager to get out of the populated area as quickly as possible. Thirty minutes later, they were entering New London, Missouri, with less than a quarter tank of gas in the truck.

"We need to stop and refuel soon." Ayden gestured to the fuel gauge on the dash.

Mueller consulted his paper map of the state. "Take this next exit."

Ayden steered the old Ford off the highway and onto a side road.

"There." Mueller pointed to an empty gravel lot close to the main road.

Ayden pulled the truck into the lot and stopped by a stand of trees. He felt the truck shift as Frank and Jacob exited the bed, fuel cans in hand. In less than five minutes, the gauge told Ayden the tank was full, and Frank and Jacob climbed back into the truck.

"We'll have to be on high alert after we get onto Highway 36." Mueller folded the map. "We will be past Monroe City and then Shelbina; both have a population of a thousand people or more. We could encounter roadblocks or bandits along that stretch of highway."

"Should we continue on the back roads, then?" Laney asked.

"I'd sure like to make up some of the time we've eaten up zigzagging through the last three states. From the map, it looks small. We could push this old girl up to its top speed of eighty miles per hour and get to Ogallala, Nebraska, by a little after dark."

"Seriously?"

"Well, more like ten or eleven o'clock with dropping Billie Jean off in Macon and then stopping to find fuel."

Laney slumped her shoulders. "So midnight, then."

Mueller patted her knee. "Probably. I'm as ready as anyone to get the heck out of this truck."

Laney twisted in his direction. "How are you feeling, Daddy?"

"Fine, honey. My back is just too old for long road trips."

"At least we aren't walking," Laney said.

"You hush your mouth!" Monica barked from the back. "Don't jinx us like that."

"Sorry, Momma." Laney chuckled over her shoulder. She turned to Ayden. "My mom is very superstitious."

Monica's voice pitched. "I am not!"

"Dad?"

"I'm staying out of this one."

"You should. You're in enough hot water, mister."

"What did I do?"

"What did I do?" she mocked.

"Hey, it wasn't my idea."

"No?"

"No!" Mueller said. "Why would I want to put myself through hell for her?"

Monica's brow knit. "I don't know. That's what I've been asking myself."

"Don't fret about it, love. In about thirty minutes, we'll drop her at her sister's or whoever lives in Macon, and you'll never see her again."

"You better hope not," Monica huffed.

Ayden steered the truck between an abandoned SUV and dump truck before crossing over and turning west onto Highway 36, east of Monroe City, Missouri. He was able to speed up to seventy miles per hour on the divided four-lane highway as it was basically deserted of abandoned vehicles.

Mueller spotted it first. "Roadblock!" he shouted, unholstering his pistol.

Ayden stomped on the brake, tossing the occupants in the pickup bed forward against the cab. "What do I do?"

"Reverse! Reverse!" Mueller shouted.

Ayden complied.

"There!" Mueller yelled. "Take that turnaround into the east-bound lane. I'll find us a route around it."

A few minutes later, Mueller directed Ayden to take the next right, and they were heading back the way they'd just come.

"Take the next right," Mueller said, consulting his map again.

Thirty miles later, Mueller directed Ayden to return to Highway 36 after having skirted the more populated towns. As they rolled into Macon, a town of over five thousand people, the streets appeared deserted. Ayden weaved through abandoned traffic and pulled to a stop at the first intersection.

Mueller rolled down his window. "Which way, Billie Jean?"

She shouted out the directions, and Ayden drove through town, turning right onto Rubey Street. He stopped at the intersection where she'd directed him, but there wasn't a yellow two-story house on the corner. There was no house at all. All he saw was an empty lot. Frank assisted Billie Jean from the bed of the truck, and the two stood in the middle of the street, staring in that direction.

"What's going on?" Monica asked, rolling down her window.

"Her momma's house is gone," Frank said over his shoulder.

Billie Jean dropped to her knees, placed her head on the pavement, and sobbed.

"We can't stay here, Frank. We're exposed," Mueller called to him.

"What do you want me to do?"

"Pick her up and put her in the truck," Mueller said.

Ayden glanced in the rearview mirror, expecting a response from Monica. Instead, she rolled up her window and stared straight ahead. As Frank assisted Billie Jean back to the vehicle, Monica wiped a tear from her cheek. Ayden wasn't sure if they were mad tears at having to continue their journey with her or if she felt empathy for the poor woman.

No one inside the cab spoke as Ayden turned the vehicle around and returned to the highway. Two hours later, as they approached St. Joseph, Missouri, Mueller broke the silence.

"Take a right up here!" Mueller said, urgency in his tone. "We're going to cross the Missouri River at Rulo."

Mueller was navigating. He had the map and had selected the route, so Ayden didn't question the change in direction. As he slowed to take the turn, he spotted why Mueller changed his mind.

Sandy brown-colored military vehicles stretched out as far as the eye could see—and they were heading their way.

"They're ours, right?" Serenity asked, leaning forward with her hand on the back of Mueller's seat.

"They're ours," Mueller said.

As Ayden made the turn, the US military convoy raced east in the opposite lanes. "You think they're heading to the front lines?" he asked.

"I hope so," Mueller said. "They could be just out on patrols. Or they could be stationed here to control the bridge. Whiteman Air Force Base is two hours south of here. Fort Leonard Wood—an Army base—is about four hours. I expected to see a military presence in the state, sooner or later."

"Why can't we cross into Kansas from here, then?" Serenity asked.

"The last time I tried to cross a bridge, they took my vehicle."

"Rulo it is then," Ayden said, steering the old Ford north onto Highway 29 and away from the military convoy.

TWENTY-THREE

Ayden

Highway 59
St. Joseph, Missouri
Day Twenty-Five

Ayden glanced down at the gas gauge as they moved north to avoid the US Forces at St. Joseph, Missouri. "We need fuel. We're way under a quarter tank."

"Let's get away from this populated area before we stop," Mueller said. "Once we're away from buildings and houses, we'll look for an abandoned vehicle."

Surprisingly, there were few vehicles on the northbound lanes of Highway 59. The ones they passed were big rigs or other diesel trucks. The few cars on the road were already empty, and they'd driven forty-five miles without passing a town.

While crossing Little Tariko Creek, Ayden spotted the very long train that sat on the tracks alongside the westbound lane— likely carrying grain from the fields of Kansas and Nebraska. Ayden wondered how many millions of tons of it sat on idle trains like that one. As the road veered left close to the tracks, he began to think of other commodities that were shipped by rail.

Grains, for sure. What about petroleum products?

How great would it be to find a whole freight car full of canned foods?

He recalled seeing a half-mile-long train filled with military vehicles once. He chuckled to himself, imagining the look on Mia's face if they were to roll up in a Humvee. The boys would love it. The closer they got to Wyoming, the more anxious Ayden was growing to see them.

As they approached the Fortescue, Missouri, sign, the fuel light came on, and then the low fuel warning system began to chime.

"What do you think?" Ayden asked, pointing to the turn for the town. "It's that or walk the next nine hundred miles."

Mueller turned in his seat. "Monica, wake up, love."

"I'm awake," she said, stirring. She twisted and pushed open the back sliding glass. "We're getting fuel in this next town."

"Heads on a swivel," Mueller called out, cranking down his side window.

"Roger that," Frank said.

Almost immediately, they passed a farmer standing at the door to his barn. His hand raised in a wave. Mueller returned the gesture.

"Population thirty-two!" Serenity said. "I don't know about this. How are we going to find fuel here?"

"We're going to try to buy some," Mueller said.

Monica's brows knit. "With what?"

"Gold," Serenity said.

Ayden shot him a glance. "You think that's wise? If they find out we have gold and no fuel to escape, they may just kill us for it."

"No one is going to risk their lives for gold anymore," Monica said.

"Then why would they trade fuel for it?" Serenity asked.

"They may not. Depends on how we approach the trade," Mueller said.

"I can't wait to hear this," Monica snarked.

"Shouldn't we turn around and talk to that farmer, then?" Ayden asked. "I bet he has fuel for all those tractors."

Mueller shook his head. "Just diesel, likely. And farmers are smart and savvy—not easily tricked by city folks like us."

They continued into the small town, passing tiny houses that, from the looks of it, were likely built in the 1940s or 1950s. Mueller gestured, and Ayden veered right onto a narrow gravel road.

"What are we looking for, exactly?" Ayden asked.

"I'll know when I see it."

As they approached an older two-story home with its porch leaning, Mueller leaned forward. "There!"

Ayden pulled to a stop. The lawn was littered with cars up on jacks, and a huge pile of parts and junk was stacked next to a run-down detached garage.

A middle-aged man dressed in blue coveralls stepped out onto the porch, shielding his eyes from the glare of the mid-afternoon sun. "Can I help you folks?" He perused the occupants in the bed of the truck as he descended the rickety steps to his lawn.

"Yes!" Mueller said.

The guy's gaze shifted back to Mueller.

"Yes, maybe." Mueller opened his truck door.

"Tyson!" Monica said as he placed his right leg outside the vehicle.

"Just keep your heads on a swivel," Mueller said in a hushed tone. "We'll be out of here in a flash."

"Tyson, I don't like this at all."

Mueller didn't respond to his wife and continued to ease himself out of the pickup. He stood facing the man with his injured left arm bent across his abdomen.

"Where you folks from?" the man asked, stopping in the middle of his lawn.

"Pennsylvania," Mueller said.

"You're a long way from home. What ya doing here in Fortescue?"

"Passing through. Just trying to make it to Wyoming."

"That's a far piece to travel—especially these days."

"It is for sure—especially with all the gas stations closed."

The man's eyebrows shot up. "Ah, I see. You need gas."

"We do. Do you have any to spare? Any amount would help us get farther down the road."

The man scratched his head and glanced back at the detached garage. "I don't know. It's not like I can run into Rulo and buy more."

"I understand that, but I hoped you might be willing to trade for some."

The man cocked his head to one side. "What do you have that's as valuable as fuel?"

"Well, what do you need?" Mueller asked.

The man's gaze flicked to the bed of the truck, then back toward his house. A sly smile appeared on his lips. "That's a nice-looking group you got there. Nice-looking, indeed."

"Give the man Billie Jean," Monica said.

"Mom!" Laney glanced back. "Shhh."

"I don't reckon you got food to spare—or alcohol?" the man said.

"No, but I've got cash you could buy some with."

"Cash ain't worth nothing now. The stores ain't taking it no more. They're only taking something edible to trade or something useful for trade these days."

"What about gold? Are they taking that?" Mueller asked.

Ayden felt the truck shift and glanced into the rearview mirror. Frank had traded places with Billie Jean and moved toward the tailgate, clutching his pistol at his side.

The man's eyes widened. "Gold, you say!" Once more, he scratched the back of his head. "Don't rightly know about that. Nobody out this way got any gold." Once more, he glanced back at his house. "But that fella at the bar in Rulo used to own the pawnshop in town. I bet he'd take gold." He made eye contact with Mueller. "Don't know if he's got any gasoline, though. You'd have to check with him about that."

"At the bar, you say?" Mueller pursed his lips. "Not sure we have enough fuel to make it to Rulo. We're pretty much on fumes."

"You're hoping I'll trade you gold for fuel?"

"I am."

The man started to look back again, but movement in the bed of the truck caught his attention.

Frank climbed over the tailgate and set a gas can down on the ground.

"Keep your eyes on the upstairs windows, Laney," Ayden said, holding his pistol between his legs out of the man's sight.

"I got the door to that garage," Monica said.

"I'll take the side yard and watch for anyone coming around from the back," Serenity said, shifting toward her door.

In the rearview mirror, Ayden watched Jane push Finn's head down. She'd already slid the strap of her rifle's sling over her head, and the weapon rested in her lap. She was facing the opposite side of the street with her hand gripping the rifle's stock. Everyone in the truck was on high alert.

"Show me this gold, and I'll consider it."

"Show me the gasoline," Mueller said.

He stepped back, gesturing to a line of fuel cans sitting between his house and the garage.

"Those look empty," Mueller said.

"A couple of 'em have gas in 'em."

"How much you willing to give me?"

"Depends. How much gold ya got to pay for it?"

Mueller inched his right hand toward his pocket, but the man jumped back, eyes wide. "It's in my pocket. I can show you."

"How do I know you ain't gonna shoot me and take my gas?"

"You don't. You have to trust me, just like I have to trust that woman in the window up there isn't going to fire at me."

The man turned and glanced up at the second-story window. He waved his hand in the air, and the curtain moved.

"She can't shoot you," the man said, returning his focus to Mueller and the occupants of the truck. "She ain't even got no bullets in the dang thang."

"Let's get this deal done then." Frank stepped onto the man's lawn with the fuel can in hand. "So we can get on down the road and out of your hair."

The man turned toward the garage. "I only got about two gallons left. Don't have nothing that'll run, so I guess I could trade ya." He glanced back at Frank. "I'd need to see that gold first, though."

Mueller reached into his pocket and produced one shiny gold coin. He held it up so the man could see it.

"How do I know it's real?"

"You got a strong magnet in that shop of yours?"

"I might."

"Pure gold is not ferromagnetic due to its lack of iron, nickel, and cobalt," Finn explained, crawling over to the side of the bed and draping his arms over the side. "But you need a strong neodymium magnet to test it."

The man raised one eyebrow.

"He's right. Pure gold isn't magnetic." Mueller stepped toward the man.

Laney and Monica exited the truck as Mueller and Frank followed the man into his garage to test the gold coin.

Ayden kept his hand on the ignition, ready to start the truck and flee if anything happened.

Moments later, Mueller, Frank, and the man returned. They were smiling and joking as they approached the truck.

"His hands were wrapped up in the reins so tight the feller couldn't get his hand free," the man was saying as he flipped the gold coin between his fingers. "That horse took off like a scalded dog, bouncing the poor ole boy's head against the dirt halfway to the barn by the time he wiggled his hand free. He ain't been right in the head ever since."

"I would suppose not." Mueller chuckled.

Frank rushed over and poured gasoline into the fuel tank as Laney and Monica climbed back into the truck.

"Mexico, you say!" The man ran a hand through his long, greasy hair. "Ya know, I think I'd rather stay here and fight commies than go all that way to Mexico and deal with the cartels."

"I feel the same," Mueller said. "Just thought I'd let you know what you might be in for and give you the option now before they're on your doorstep."

"I appreciate that, Mueller. I hope you guys reach your destination unharmed."

"Thanks, Charlie," Mueller said, climbing into the truck.

With the gas gauge now reading a one-quarter tank full, Ayden drove back toward the highway. Before reaching it, there was a rap on the back window. Monica opened it, and Jane's voice came through.

"Can we pull over by that tractor? Billie Jean needs to water the daisies."

"No!" Monica snapped. "She can hold it or wet her pants."

Mueller sighed heavily. "Pull over there, Ayden. Let everyone who needs to take a bathroom break so we don't have to stop again until after we find more fuel."

Ayden rolled forward and stopped beside a massive tractor that had tires as tall as the pickup's cab. All the ladies, excluding Monica, exited and walked to the other side of the tractor. Mueller, Frank, and Jacob relieved themselves a short distance away from the passenger side of the truck. When the ladies returned, they took another minute or two to retrieve bottled water and snacks from packs.

Five minutes after leaving Fortescue, Ayden pulled the Ford F350 back onto the highway, heading west toward the Missouri-Nebraska state lines.

The wind was whipping through the cab as Ayden pushed the truck at top speed. His mind was on Mia's ranch and the wide-open spaces of Wyoming as they drew near the end of the train.

Suddenly, from out of nowhere, a jacked-up, older model red and white Dodge truck bounced over the tracks from a side street and barreled out in front of them.

"Watch it!" Laney screamed, gripping the dash.

TWENTY-FOUR

Ayden

Highway 59
St. Joseph, Missouri
Day Twenty-Five

"Ayden!" Laney screamed.

He yanked the wheel to the left just in time to miss rear-ending the custom-lifted truck. The other driver hadn't even stopped to look for cross traffic, and with the train parked on the tracks, he wouldn't have seen their Ford.

Ayden's grip on the steering wheel tightened as he veered into the left-hand lane to avoid a collision. He floored the accelerator, the engine roaring in response as they sped past the truck. Glancing over, Ayden caught sight of the driver—his face was smug, lips curled into a gleeful smile that seemed to mock their near-miss.

The man accelerated again, and as he pulled up alongside them and jockeyed for position, Ayden now noticed the person in the passenger seat. It was the man who'd sold them the fuel just minutes earlier.

"What the hell?" Mueller spat.

"What's he doing?" Monica asked, her tone laced with panic. "I knew flashing that gold was going to get us in trouble!"

Ayden pulled ahead and pegged out the speedometer, bumping over the relatively smooth, straight roadway in an effort to put distance between them and the Dodge.

"Oh, crap!" Monica said as the jacked-up truck caught up to them, nearly matching their speed.

The man from Fortescue shouted over the roar of their engines. "Pull over!"

Laney reached over Ayden and aimed her pistol at the man.

"Laney!" Mueller shouted. "Don't! We've got kids back there!"

The Dodge slowed momentarily, and Ayden seized the chance to surge ahead. He pressed the pedal down as hard as he could, urging the old Ford to give everything it had.

"Ayden!" Serenity shouted from the back as the truck sped up to catch them. Ayden glanced into the rearview mirror and then his side mirror. It was clear the people in the truck were coming after them. He glanced over as Mueller unholstered his pistol.

"Hold on! I'm going to try to outrun them," Ayden said, glancing back at Frank, who had shifted position in the truck bed, rifle at the ready.

The truck screamed and whined as Ayden pushed it past its limits. As they approached a sharp curve, the Ford swayed dangerously from side to side. Ayden's heart skipped as he checked the rearview mirror, relieved to see that Frank, although unsteady, had managed to hold on. The big guy had lost his balance and was still trying to right himself.

Laney gripped her pistol with both hands, pointing it down at the footwell, her body tense. "Ayden! They're right behind us," Monica cried out, her voice edged with urgency.

"Watch those two men in the bed. One's poking his head above its cab," Mueller said, bending to view his side mirror. "He may have a rifle. I can't tell."

Boom!

A gunshot rang out, and Ayden instinctively jerked the wheel to the left. The bullet missed, but the Dodge kept coming.

"Ayden, do something!" Serenity yelled.

Frank responded with gunfire of his own, though Ayden couldn't tell if his shots found their mark. The Dodge kept on their tail, relentless.

Boom!

Boom!

More shots. The sound of bullets striking metal was terrifyingly loud, prompting Frank to duck behind the tailgate. Ayden swerved from lane to lane in a frantic attempt to dodge the incoming fire.

Mueller leaned out his window, returning fire, while Monica did the same.

"Go faster! Go faster, Ayden!" Serenity yelled.

"I can't! The pedal is on the floor!" Ayden's voice was a mix of frustration and fear as he glanced between the road ahead and the mirrors.

"They just keep coming," Monica shouted, reloading.

The men in the bed of their truck struggled to maintain balance as the vehicle accelerated and steered into the eastbound lane to avoid Frank's barrage of bullets.

Mueller dropped his pistol's magazine. "Laney!"

As she bent to pull a spare magazine from the bag at her feet, the back glass shattered, sending glass into the cab and leaving a spiderwebbed hole in the windshield on Mueller's side. It remained intact—at least for the moment.

Monica took aim at the lifted Dodge through her window opening, but before she could get off a shot, they fired again. Everyone in the Ford ducked, and the Dodge accelerated ahead of them a few hundred feet. Ayden had to mash the brakes to avoid rear-ending their attackers. As the Dodge in front of him stopped in the roadway and the shooters in the bed took aim, Ayden stomped on the gas pedal, swerved into the westbound lane, and bolted past them.

Boom!

Boom!

"Frank!" Monica shouted through the shattered back glass. Relief washed over Ayden as the big guy popped his head up. "Anyone hit?"

"We're good!" Jane yelled back.

As Ayden's eyes snapped back to the road, he saw an immediate crisis—both lanes ahead were blocked by abandoned vehicles. He had mere seconds to react.

"Hold on!" he shouted.

With a firm grasp, Ayden clenched the steering wheel, his muscles taut as he slammed down on the brakes. The tires emitted a high-pitched screech, their rubber clawing at the asphalt as the truck surged forward from the abrupt deceleration. Monica, unprepared for the sudden stop, flew forward, her forearm crashing into the back of Ayden's headrest.

"Ouch!" she cried out from the impact, but Ayden's attention was riveted on the rearview mirror.

Behind them, the Dodge that had been tailing them also attempted to brake. Its tires smoked under the strain as the driver fought to control the vehicle. The pickup swerved wildly, zigzagging across the road before veering off the pavement. Ayden watched, heart pounding, as two figures were ejected from the bed of the Dodge. Their bodies struck the asphalt hard just seconds before the truck careened into the ditch and rolled onto its side.

Ayden turned just in time to see the lifted pickup flip multiple times, a horrific ballet of metal and momentum before it came to rest on its side in the ditch.

"Is everyone okay?" Ayden asked as they steered onto the shoulder and maneuvered around the abandoned vehicles blocking the roadway.

"Yes." Monica twisted in her seat to peer out the shattered back window. "That was close!"

The wind whipped through the cab as Ayden sped up, putting distance between them and the jacked-up Dodge. He knew Mueller had chosen this route, hoping they could avoid danger by bypassing the major cities, but peril still seemed to await them around every turn.

TWENTY-FIVE

Ayden

Highway 159
Rulo, Nebraska
Day Twenty-Five

As they approached the bridge spanning the Missouri River, Ayden slowed the truck. "I can't see what's on the other side."

"Ease forward. Let's get a look."

"Might be safer to go around," Monica said. "Find another bridge across."

"We can't go back the way we came. He could have told others about the gold. They could be coming for us now," Mueller said.

"What do you think?" Ayden asked.

"I say we floor it, get through town as fast as possible, and don't stop for anything," Mueller said.

Ayden did just that. They approached the bridge doing sixty miles per hour. Ayden swerved around an abandoned car and crossed into Rulo, Nebraska. They'd crossed the bridge over the Missouri River, and there wasn't anyone waiting to stop them on the other side. Several men were standing around in a restaurant's parking lot, but none of them moved. Rulo had no stop signs or traffic lights to halt traffic on Highway 159, so they were in and out of the town quickly. Moments later, they were heading south to hook up with Highway 36.

A few miles out from there, in Hiawatha, Kansas, Ayden pulled to a stop beside a newer model Ford truck. He and Frank drained it of its fuel and filled the old Ford's fuel tank. Afterward, due to there being virtually no vehicles on the roadway, they were able to maintain highway speed and made excellent time across Kansas, even with having to skirt several towns.

The two-lane blacktop of US Highway 36 stretched out from east to west across northern Kansas, running through a bunch of "Norman Rockwell Americana" small towns outside of those, offering almost nothing of interest to catch the eye. Field after field of wheat, corn, soybeans, and even cotton stretched out before them.

"This is what they're after?" Laney asked, gesturing to the fields on either side of the roadway.

"People have to eat. The Midwest fed a third of the world with what they grow here. With drought and the wars Russia and China were already engaged in Ukraine and Taiwan, skirmishes with India and Japan, and had their fingers in the Middle East, their population is starving. But don't be fooled. They didn't start all this to control agricultural lands here in the Midwest." Mueller gestured out his side window. "This is a bonus. They've been preparing for the Chinese Communist Party's push to level the playing field against the US and its allies. Wanting to shift that system and the global balance of power to ensure China's rise to world dominance. Power is what this is about. With the US out of the way, China is the new superpower."

"What about Russia?"

Mueller laughed. "They may think they are partners or allies, but they are no more than pawns in Beijing's chess game. If China manages to subdue our citizens, it will turn on Russia."

"What happens to us if they win?" Serenity asked.

Mueller paused before answering. He drew in a deep breath and slowly let it out. "We can't let that happen."

They grew quiet again, each no doubt pondering the repercussions of living under Chinese or Russian rule. Ayden's mind wandered. He thought about all the places he'd visited while filming his extreme sports documentaries—places like Laos, Mali, Thailand, and Venezuela, with authoritarian governments. None of those had a sophisticated social credit system like China to track and restrict the freedoms of its people, but they still had significant human rights issues.

China's method of control in the US would be brutal and deadly. Images of the drone strikes on New Eden flooded his mind. He imagined his sister, crushed under the weight of debris, calling his name. His grief was overwhelming. He pushed away the thoughts and focused on the road ahead and the prospect of reaching Wyoming. He pictured instead the moment he reunited with Mia and the boys, but too soon, anguish mixed with panic over not knowing what he might find there.

Nearly three hours later, with the fuel gauge once again low, Mueller directed Ayden to proceed slowly into Smith Center, Kansas.

"That's too risky, Ty," Monica said as Ayden let off the accelerator. "I think we should keep avoiding towns and look for fuel elsewhere."

"I disagree, love. We haven't seen a vehicle on the road in an hour. We'll burn too much fuel skirting the town, with no guarantee of finding more in time. It's too big of a risk. We can't walk from here."

Ayden pulled over as the two debated the issue, with Laney attempting to mediate between her parents. Finally, Frank appeared at Ayden's window. "How about Ayden and I take the fuel cans, run into town for fuel, and bring it back? That way, we don't risk getting the truck taken or attracting too much attention. We can slip in and out."

Aren't we tempting fate trying this again? Ayden thought. It hadn't worked out so well for them back at the auto salvage yard in Shoals, Indiana. He'd almost had to shoot an old man.

"I like that idea better," Monica said. "Less risk to the children. They've been traumatized enough."

Although Finn seemed to weather it all like a little trooper, Ayden was sure the kid would carry lifelong scars from the experience thus far. If he could avoid adding to his trauma and keep Finn, Jacob, and the others safe, it was worth risking a deadly confrontation in town.

"I'll do it," Ayden said. "I'll go with Frank to get gas."

Frank grabbed the fuel cans, and the two set off toward town. Their first stop was a business right off the highway, with a parking lot full of new tractors and heavy equipment. The only gasoline-powered vehicle—a newer model SUV—was already empty.

Ayden and Frank continued toward town, checking cars in the parking lots of restaurants and businesses, but they came up empty each time.

"Someone's taken all the fuel on this end of town," Frank said.

They were forced farther and farther from their truck and friends, avoiding homes because they didn't want to risk an encounter with their occupants. Despite Ayden's reservations, they ventured downtown, taking Main Street south past empty shops and businesses, checking vehicles as they went, and finding them all empty.

"There!" Frank said in a hushed tone. He chopped the air and led Ayden down an alley behind what appeared to be a bar. They stopped beside a newer model SUV, and Ayden crawled beneath it. "It doesn't look like this one's been touched yet."

Frank handed him the screwdriver and hammer and then slid the pan underneath. Ayden created the hole, and fuel splashed into the pan for a few seconds before stopping. "I was wrong. The tank was almost empty, Frank."

Frank pulled out the pan and poured it into their fuel can as Ayden climbed out from beneath the SUV.

"How much did we get?"

"Less than a gallon. We need to keep looking. I don't want to go back until we have at least ten," Frank said.

Ayden dusted himself off and scanned the area for more vehicles.

Frank continued walking another twenty feet and stopped. He dropped to a crouch behind a trash dumpster, waving his hand for Ayden to seek cover as well.

Ayden moved to his right toward a small fenced-in area that contained a storage shed. The doors were padlocked. Ayden pressed his back against the fence, brought his rifle up, and shouldered it, listening for whatever Frank had been concerned about. And then he heard it—the roar of an engine, possibly a generator, along with country music and laughter. The voices were faint but unmistakable.

Frank gestured for him to stay put and then disappeared around the garbage bin. A moment later, he returned, waving Ayden forward. "They're running a generator in that bar over there."

He nodded in that direction. "Means they have fuel. It could be diesel, but let's hope it's gasoline."

"It would make sense it's gas-fueled with all the vehicles they've emptied around here."

"I hope we're that lucky. Wouldn't it be easier to take a couple of fuel cans and disappear than to keep crawling under cars and coming up empty?"

Ayden agreed since he was the one doing the crawling, but he doubted those folks had just left cans of fuel sitting around for the taking. They'd have it hidden, like in the locked shed. He glanced back at the portable building—or guarded. "Won't they post a guard on their fuel to keep people like us from stealing it?"

"Maybe, but I didn't see any. Let's go check it out."

Frank rose and set off running in a crouch. Ayden followed him around the side of a building. When they reached the front, Frank halted him with a raised fist. "Would you look at that? They're not at all concerned about folks stealing from them."

"What?" Ayden asked, stepping alongside him.

"See that pickup parked in front of the bar down the street?"

"Yeah!" It was an older model GMC.

"Check out all those red cans in the bed."

"What the..."

"I know, right? It's like they collected all that just for us."

"They're probably empty. They wouldn't leave full cans out like that, right?"

"Won't know until we check," Frank said.

Ayden was torn. Three weeks ago, he would have never considered stealing fuel from another man's truck. And now, even though his moral compass had taken a beating of late, he still didn't like the idea—for one, it was dangerous. The truck was parked right in front of the bar. Anyone who was looking out the windows or standing in the doorway would see them.

"I'll run and grab two cans while you cover me from there..." Frank chopped his hand in the air and gestured to a spot across the street with a full view of the door to the bar.

Ayden took two steps toward the street and stopped. "Maybe we should keep looking. This is—"

"I'm tired, and the longer our folks sit on the side of the roadway like that, the more likely it is someone will spot them. We have to get this fuel and return to the others. We don't have time to check every vehicle in town."

Ayden didn't like this setup, but Frank was right. Their group was vulnerable out there on the highway. If they had to flee to avoid some attacker, he and Frank might be stranded in Smith Center. Then he'd be forced to walk all the way to Wyoming. They had to take risks—that was just what life had become. They either exploited opportunities like the one presented to them in this instance or risked the lives of those counting on them. If he was forced to choose between whoever was inside that bar, using the fuel to run a generator so they could listen to music and keep their beer cold, or the chance to get Laney, Finn, Serenity, and the others to the safety he believed awaited them in Wyoming—he'd choose his friends each time. "Okay, I'll cover you."

"You post up there at the corner of that barbershop and monitor the door."

"Got it." Ayden took off in a sprint and stopped on the opposite side of the street at the corner between two buildings. From there, he watched as Frank crept toward the bed of the pickup. He stopped at the passenger side door and peered inside. Frank glanced over at Ayden, jabbed a finger in the direction of the driver's seat, and mouthed something.

Ayden didn't understand what he was saying. Frank then made a driving gesture. Ayden's heart skipped a beat as he realized what Frank intended to do. "No!" Ayden mouthed back. He knew there was no way Frank could climb inside the truck, start it, and then drive away without alerting the bar's patrons.

A second later, Frank's hand was on the door handle. He eased it open, his gaze fixed on the door to the bar. Ayden wanted to run and stop him, but by then, it was too late. He was inside, sliding in behind the wheel. Ayden trained his crosshairs on the bar's door as Frank cranked over the engine. Ayden tensed, preparing to shoot whoever poked their head through the opening, but no one did.

Frank put the truck in Reverse, backed out quickly, and stopped in front of Ayden. "Get in. Hurry!" he gritted.

As Ayden took his first step toward the truck, an overweight man wearing shorts and a pair of Crocs ran from the bar, lifting a handgun as if in slow motion.

Boom!

Frank leaned to open Ayden's door just as the man fired the first round.

The sound echoed off the buildings as Ayden tossed his pack into the vehicle and then dove into the passenger seat.

Boom!

Boom!

More rounds peppered the truck. Ayden spun to check the fuel cans in the back, afraid one of the rounds might ignite the fuel and blow them sky high.

"Move! Move! Move!" he shouted over the roar of the engine and the sound of the man's pistol.

The truck hesitated slightly as Frank stomped the gas but eventually took off as the man emptied his weapon's magazine into the driver's side of the vehicle.

TWENTY-SIX

Ayden

Full Circle Lounge
Smith Center, Kansas
Day Twenty-Five

At the next intersection, Frank yanked the wheel hard to the left and sped past homes. Ayden scanned ahead and down the side streets, expecting the owner of the truck to pop out at any moment.

They were forced to make several more turns as they weaved through residential streets. At a four-way stop just blocks from the highway, Frank put the truck into Park, leaving it idling.

"I think you should drive," Frank said, clutching his shoulder. He removed his hand to reach for the door handle, revealing a bright crimson stain covering his hand and shirt.

"You're hit!" Ayden yelled.

"It's a through and through. I need to take care of it while you drive. We need to get away from here in case that guy has friends."

"Let me get you some water and—"

"Ayden, just drive!" Frank barked.

Ayden exited the truck, leaving his door open for Frank, and ran around the back. He could smell the strong odor of gasoline as he rounded the back bumper. He jumped behind the wheel as Frank slid into the passenger seat with a groan. Ayden raced through town and turned east upon finally reaching the highway. He floored the gas pedal, but seventy-five miles per hour was all the old pickup would do. Frank cried out as the truck hit potholes in the pavement.

"Frank, let me pull over and put pressure on your wound," Ayden pleaded.

"I'm already doing that. You just worry about keeping this truck on the road. And if you could miss a pothole or two, that would be great."

"Frank, you're losing too much blood. Let me help you stop it before you bleed out. Now, I'm pulling over to take care of your wound." He yanked the wheel and whipped into the factory parking lot, stopping behind a tractor-trailer rig out of sight of the road.

Ayden jumped out and ran around to the passenger side, yanked open the door, then ripped the fabric of Frank's T-shirt. Frank gritted his teeth and cried out as Ayden dug his finger into the hole in Frank's back, searching for the exit wound.

"I don't feel anything. It must have gone through," Ayden said, applying pressure with the palm of his hand.

Frank fell forward. Ayden laid him back onto the seat and retrieved a bottle of water from his pack. He sat him up and made him drink half the bottle before he allowed him to lie back down. Ayden grabbed his backpack from the bed of the stolen truck and put it on the ground just outside the passenger door. He unzipped the pack and pulled out the gauze and bandages, then pushed the dressing into each side of the hole and applied as much pressure on each one as he could.

"Hold this," Ayden said, placing Frank's hand on the wound just below his left clavicle.

Ayden poked more gauze into the hole in Frank's back and

wrapped the bandage under his arm and across the wound in the front.

After he had finished dressing the wound, he said, "Drink the rest of this water."

Frank looked pale, his skin was clammy, and he had lost far too much blood.

He needs a hospital and likely a blood transfusion, or he isn't going to make it.

They had to get back to the others. Perhaps Mueller would know what to do. Maybe he had contacts in Kansas who could treat his friend. Ayden started the truck and got back on the road, his gaze bouncing between the road ahead and the rearview mirror, expecting to encounter trouble before reaching their group.

Ayden blasted the truck's horn as he raced toward Mueller's Ford, waving his left hand out the driver's side window, not wanting Laney or the others to think they were a threat and begin firing upon them. Ayden stomped the brakes and stopped several hundred feet away. "Hold on, Frank. Mueller will know what to do," Ayden said as he threw open his door and jumped from the vehicle. "It's me! Don't shoot! It's me and Frank!" he yelled, waving his hands over his head, praying a bullet didn't rip through him any second.

Laney and Monica were the first to reach them. Monica yanked open Frank's door and began working to stop the bleeding as Mueller hurried to him as fast as he was able.

Ayden stepped back to allow them to work on their friend. They scanned the road to the west, looking for the truck's owner or anyone who might have heard him honking.

"Where the hell did you get the truck?" Mueller asked as he approached, rifle shouldered and eyes scanning the horizon.

"In town. There's fuel cans in the bed." Ayden gestured to them without taking his eyes off the highway.

"How many shooters?" Mueller said, moving around to the passenger side and peering inside at his friend.

"Just one—that I saw."

"How's he doing?" Mueller asked.

"He's losing too much blood."

"I'll be fine. Let's get the hell out of here before trouble comes for us again," Frank said, his voice barely a hoarse whisper.

"He's right, Monica. We have to move him."

"Ayden, pull that truck up next to mine and help me put him in the back." Mueller turned to Laney. "You and Mom fill the tank and put the rest in the bed."

Ayden jumped in behind the wheel as Laney and Monica climbed into the bed. Mueller began walking back as Ayden took off. Minutes later, Frank was back in Mueller's Ford, and its fuel tank was full.

"Should we turn around and take another route?"

"Hell no. Floor this puppy and get us out of here," Mueller said, chopping the air with his hand.

TWENTY-SEVEN

Mia Christiansen

Rock Springs Fairgrounds
Rock Springs, Wyoming
Day Twenty-Four

The journey to Rock Springs had started with a mix of apprehension and excitement. Even though the US soldiers said the Russian military's advance into their area had been stopped, she couldn't help but worry.

Dirk drove the old Ford truck pulling a cattle trailer loaded with two robust steers and all the necessary equipment for butchering. Mia, seated beside her mother in the rear, discussed potential trades while keeping a close eye on her boys and the landscape.

Arriving in Rock Springs, the scene was almost festive. Tables lined the streets, each laden with goods ranging from homemade jams to handcrafted tools. The Christiansens quickly set up their makeshift corral and butchering station. As Neil and Dirk processed the first steer, the aroma of fresh meat attracted a crowd eager to trade.

Mia managed the trading with her sons Carter and Luke helping, while little Xavier clung to his grandmother, Melody, who kept a watchful eye on the proceedings. The community came together, laughing and sharing stories, creating a lively atmosphere filled with the hum of bartering.

However, the festive mood shattered at the distant sound of engines. Mia stopped in her tracks, straining to listen. Panic coiled around her throat as she realized what it was. She tried to scream, but no words came out. Desperation took over, and she sprinted toward her children, who were several feet away. She gathered them into her arms just as Russian soldiers rolled into town in armored vehicles.

Panic ensued as people screamed and scrambled for cover while gunfire erupted.

"Get down!" Mia shouted to her boys, pulling them closer as chaos enveloped the market.

Tom and Eric, the cowboys, reacted instantly. They drew their pistols, taking cover behind their truck and firing at the advancing soldiers. Despite their efforts, both were quickly overwhelmed and fell under a hail of bullets.

"Move, move!" Neil yelled, grabbing Mia and the boys and rushing them toward a nearby alley. Melody followed closely, her eyes wide with fear.

Russian soldiers swarmed the area, rounding up the market attendees with ruthless efficiency. Some residents fought back, only to be cut down. The town leaders were forcibly separated and led away under heavy guard.

"Please, just leave us be!" a woman pleaded as a soldier pushed her in the direction of the buses.

"No talking! Move!" a Russian commander barked, his accent thick and his voice cold and commanding. He gestured aggressively with his rifle, herding the frightened crowd.

Mia and her family were among those pushed toward the buses. As they stumbled along, Mia held her sons tightly, whispering reassurances even as tears streamed down her face. Dirk tried to resist, pushing back against the soldiers, but was quickly subdued and dragged onto the bus.

"Please, don't do this!" Mia cried out, reaching for Dirk as he was taken away.

Inside the bus, the mood was somber. The silence was only broken by the soft sobs of those around her. Mia sat with her family, her mind racing with fear and anger. How could this be happening? What would become of them?

As the bus doors slammed shut, the Russian commander ordered his men to confiscate the beef from the Christiansens' corral. "Load it up! We need these supplies," he commanded, overseeing the loading of the beef into a military truck.

The engine roared to life, and as Rock Springs faded into the distance, Mia felt a deep despair. The road ahead was uncertain, each mile taking them farther from everything they knew.

"Mom, what's going to happen to us?" Carter asked, his voice small and scared.

Mia squeezed his hand, fighting back her own fear. "I don't know, honey. But we'll stick together, no matter what."

The bus rumbled on, carrying them toward an unknown fate, leaving behind a town now silent except for the echo of departing military vehicles and the cries of those left behind.

TWENTY-EIGHT

Mueller

Highway 36
Smith Center, Kansas
Day Twenty-Five

The old Ford F350 rattled along the empty highway, each bump in the road jarring Mueller's battered and worn-out body. He sat bolt upright, his hand resting against the window as the landscape of Kansas rolled past in a blur of subdued colors and fading light. The horizon was a mix of golden hues and the long shadows of dusk, giving the flat, expansive fields a sober tone.

Next to him, Laney sat silent, her eyes fixed on the road ahead, her thoughts unreadable. In the back seat, Monica and Serenity were just as quiet, their mood somber.

Finally breaking the silence, Ayden turned toward Mueller, his expression solemn under the burden of what had just transpired. "Mueller, about what happened back there…" His voice trailed off for a moment as if gathering his thoughts.

Mueller turned, his features taut with concern, nodding for Ayden to continue.

Ayden cleared his throat. "We found a spot that looked promising for fuel," Ayden began, his hands tight on the steering wheel, eyes fixed on the road. "There was this bar off Main Street. They were running a generator. We heard loud music, people laughing...didn't seem like they were worried about much."

Mueller's jaw clenched. "Seems like a wasteful use of fuel."

"They'd taken it from every vehicle we came across. It was as if they were just living it up, partying without a care in the world."

"Doesn't sound like they were concerned about anyone stealing the generator or the fuel," Monica said.

"It was just sitting there in the back of an old GMC. Cans lined up like ducks." Ayden paused for a moment. He sighed heavily and then continued. "Frank thought it was our best chance. We needed that fuel."

Mueller's eyes narrowed, piecing together the outcome. "So you went for it."

Ayden nodded. "Frank covered me as I ran across the street so I'd have a full view of the door and front of the bar. He moved toward the truck and noticed the keys in the ignition. Before I knew it, he was inside, cranking the thing over. He backed up and threw open the door for me."

"And they came out shooting?" Mueller's voice was low, bracing for the answer.

Ayden swallowed hard. "The guy who ran out—he was armed. Didn't hesitate. Frank...he got us out, but not before the guy unloaded his pistol into the truck." The guilt was palpable in Ayden's voice, his gaze flickering to the rearview mirror where Frank lay in the bed of the truck in grave condition.

Mueller absorbed the story, his face softening.

"He wasn't afraid to risk everything," Ayden said, his eyes meeting Mueller's. "He didn't think twice about it."

Mueller leaned back and focused on the road ahead, but his mind was clearly on Frank, the friend who had once again put his life on the line for theirs. A heavy sigh escaped him as he processed the reality of their situation—this brutal, unending road they were on.

As the truck rumbled westward, night settled over the plains, casting a heavy blanket of darkness that seemed to reflect Mueller's inner turmoil. The road ahead was lit only by the truck's headlights, slicing through the night like a solitary beacon of hope. The hum of the engine was a constant reminder of their ongoing journey—a journey marked by unimaginable loss and relentless despair.

Mueller sat in the passenger's seat, staring out the windshield. He couldn't shake the feeling of guilt that gnawed at his soul. He had thought he was prepared. He had trained, gathered stockpiles of food, supplies, weapons, and ammunition. He had built a fortress and gathered a community of people he cared about inside it. But it hadn't been enough. A PLA drone strike had obliterated the compound in an instant. Bombs had rained down, turning their sanctuary into a smoldering ruin within seconds. The fortress that was supposed to protect them had become their tomb. Everyone but Mueller had perished.

The weight of that realization was crushing. He had let them all down—his friends who had become more like family, his wife, Monica, who had believed in his vision, and the innocent lives he had sworn to protect. The guilt was overwhelming, suffocating him.

As they drove through the endless night, Mueller's mind replayed the events over and over, each detail a dagger to his heart. He remembered the sound of the explosions, the sight of the flames consuming everything they had built, and the cries of those he couldn't save. He had promised them safety, and he had failed. The burden of that failure was almost too much to bear.

Ayden had lost his sister in the chaos, and Mueller could see the pain etched on his face. Serenity sat in the back, her eyes filled with sorrow that spoke of losing her father.

And now Frank, who had always been more like a brother, was

fighting for his life, and there was nothing Mueller could do but pray. The sense of helplessness was unbearable.

Anxious to avoid conflict with residents, Ayden maneuvered the old Ford around several small Kansas towns. Mueller kept stealing glances over his shoulder as they drove, each time sending a prayer to the heavens and hoping for a miracle similar to the one that had brought Laney back to him and rescued Keith and Serenity in Clairton.

Three agonizing hours later, as they drew near Bird City, Kansas, Jane's urgent tapping on the window shattered the oppressive silence. Ayden immediately pulled into a secluded grain elevator parking lot, where they all exited to check on Frank.

Ayden, his face contorted with concern, wrapped his arm around Finn's shoulders. At the boy's side, his dog nestled close. Jane, Sadie, and Serenity formed a small, tight circle nearby, each wearing expressions of deep sorrow mixed with a fierce resolve. Monica and Laney, unable to contain their emotions, wept quietly as Mueller climbed into the truck's bed.

His ex-wife, Billie Jean, placed Frank's hand on his chest and moved back to allow Mueller room to approach his friend.

Sitting beside Frank, Mueller took his bloody hand, feeling the life faintly pulsing through his veins. "Frank, we're here, man. Just hold on," Mueller entreated.

Frank turned his head slightly, his eyes flickering with a mix of pain and resolve. "Tyson," he murmured, his voice a raspy shadow of its usual strength. "Keep fighting…for freedom. And put some whoop-ass on those commies for me."

Mueller nodded, choking back tears. "I will, Frank. I promise you, we're gonna make them pay. Make them all pay!"

Frank's grip loosened, his breaths became shallower, and in the quiet of the Kansas plains, he took his last breath.

Rage overwhelmed Mueller as he climbed down from the tailgate. He paced around the parking lot, cursing at the sky, at the fate that had led them to this moment. After a while, Monica approached him, her presence a calming force as always. "Tyson, Frank fought bravely. He wouldn't want you to lose yourself to this anger."

Taking a deep breath, Mueller nodded slowly, his fists clenched at his sides. "We'll take the fight to them, Monica. I swear! For Frank. For all of us."

While Mueller and Monica took a moment to grieve, Ayden and Laney slipped away. Moments later, they returned and approached.

"Dad," Laney said. "We found a place…" Her voice cracked.

"It's a pond nearby," Ayden added. "I'm sorry. It's the best we could find—unless you'd like for me to go into town and find a shovel?"

"No! We need to avoid any more towns. Frank loved the water and fishing." Mueller chuckled. "He'd think it was funny that his body became fish food."

Frank was like that. He'd found humor in even the most macabre situations. Mueller was proud to have called him a friend.

They gently moved Frank's body from the truck and, under the witness of a starlit sky, placed him into the pond. Afterward, and with heavy hearts, they returned to the truck. As they drove away, leaving Bird City and his best friend behind, Mueller felt an overwhelming sense of dread. The road to Ogallala and, eventually, Wyoming loomed ahead, every mile filled with challenges. He knew that once they reached their destination, the fight for survival would be far from over. Life in the apocalypse—even if they escaped the ever-present threat of war—would continue to be filled with death and hardship.

Twenty minutes later, they passed over into Nebraska, and again, the land stretched out in crops of corn, wheat, and other grains. Mueller's mind drifted, and hours passed before they approached Ogallala, Nebraska.

Ayden pulled onto the shoulder just before the on-ramp to Interstate 80. "We're getting low on fuel again. We should refill it here, away from town," Ayden said.

As he filled the truck's tank, Mueller stood guard, his rifle at the ready.

Ayden spoke up, his voice laden with guilt. "I should have done more to protect him. This is on me."

Mueller shook his head. "No, Ayden. This isn't on you. It's those damn commies and their war. We've all done what we had to do to survive. None of us were prepared for this crap." He looked toward the interstate, his mind on the resistance fighters of World War II. He felt a kinship with them now, a shared sense of purpose and sacrifice. "Once we're safe in Farson and I see my family is okay, I'm going back out there. I'll lead the resistance if I have to. We'll bring the fight to their doorstep."

Ayden nodded, his expression solemn. "We won't go down without a fight."

As they continued their journey on Interstate 80, Mueller stared out the window, his thoughts on the battles to come, the resolve to fight burning in his chest.

TWENTY-NINE

Ayden

Cheyenne I-80 Port of Entry
Cheyenne, Wyoming
Day Twenty-Five

As the group neared Cheyenne, the landscape shifted from the sprawling plains to a more militarized zone. Signs of conflict were everywhere—barricades, armored vehicles, and a heightened presence of soldiers. As they approached a checkpoint just outside the city near the Interstate 80 Port of Entry station, Ayden slowed the Ford F350, his grip tightening on the steering wheel as the bright, broad beam of flood lights nearly blinded him.

"Ayden, cut your headlights. Everyone, keep your hands where they can see them, and for goodness's sake, do not reach toward your weapon. Don't even scratch your nose. Tell the folks in the back—including Finn and Jacob. These guys have probably been through hell, just like us. We don't want to alarm them."

Ayden rolled down the window, the brisk Wyoming air cutting through the cab's stale atmosphere. He placed both hands on the steering wheel as a young soldier approached their vehicle, his expression serious yet weary.

"You have any weapons in the vehicle?" he asked, peering into the vehicle.

"Each of us, except for the kids, has a pistol and rifle," Mueller said, holding up his driver's license and concealed carry permit.

"I'm going to need you to keep your hands where I can see them. Sergeant Wilson and Private Collins are going to take those from you while we chat."

The two soldiers appeared from behind sandbags with rifles trained on the Ford. Upon reaching Ayden's door, the initial soldiers opened it and commanded him to come out. "The rest of you sit tight. We'll get to you."

Each of the truck's occupants was removed from the vehicle, searched, and their weapons taken.

"State your names and destination," the first soldier said.

"I'm Ayden Miller. We're heading to Farson, Wyoming."

The others each gave him their names, and the soldier jotted down their information. "You'll need to pull into the inspection area and submit to an interview and if you pass, we'll escort you through the city," he explained, signaling for them to pull aside.

Ayden and the others piled back into their vehicle and drove into the inspection area. After stopping in front of two more soldiers, they again exited the truck. They were led over near a small brick building, where each of them submitted to a series of questions. Over the hum of multiple generators, the soldiers asked where they were coming from, what they had seen, and whether they had spoken to anyone.

It felt like hours had passed. At one point in Ayden's interview, they stopped and called over their captain. He made Ayden start all over at the beginning, from the time he left Manhattan until reaching Pennsylvania and meeting Mueller and his folks.

"What led you to believe that it was a presidential motorcade that was targeted in the drone attack?" the young captain asked.

Ayden described the blacked-out Lincolns and SUVs he'd seen. "They had government plates," Ayden added.

"Hold tight," the captain said. "Your escort will be here soon."

Hours passed.

As he waited, another soldier, more relaxed in demeanor, approached the others, who were huddled together near the Ford. He smiled at Laney, his gaze openly appreciative, and struck up a conversation, his tone light despite the heavy artillery strapped across his chest.

"I'm Corporal Dawson. You guys together?" he asked, nodding toward Ayden with a sly grin.

Laney laughed, a light, easy sound that contrasted with the grim situation. "He's nearly twice my age." She chuckled, her tone playful.

Ayden, overhearing the exchange, couldn't help but feel a pang of realization at her words. At that moment, he felt old. Old and tired.

"You hiked the Appalachian Trail?" he asked with a broad smile on his lips.

Laney seemed interested, standing with her arms at her sides and playing with loose strands of hair. Ayden didn't blame the soldier for hitting on her. She looked beautiful even under the harsh halogen lights.

At first, she answered his questions with one-word answers and then began peppering him with her own. "What's the military doing to fight back? We heard bits and pieces on the road."

The soldier leaned closer, lowering his voice as if sharing a secret. "We've been pushing back hard. Fired nearly all our Minuteman missiles at Russia and China, but they shot most of them down with their missile defense systems. Didn't turn the tide like we hoped."

Ayden listened intently, the news settling in his stomach like a stone.

"So what's the plan now?" Laney asked.

The corporal shrugged, his face grim. "Now"—he sighed—"we're fighting on two fronts. Both coasts are under heavy pressure. Russians are pushing toward the Rockies, and we're stretched thin trying to hold them back."

Before Laney could ask another question, a convoy of military vehicles arrived to escort them. "Looks like your ride's here," Dawson said, stepping back.

The group thanked him, and with the first rays of sunrise at their backs and under the escort of heavily armed vehicles, they drove through Cheyenne. The city bore scars of conflict, with fortifications lining the streets and fighter jets roaring overhead.

As they passed the turnoff for Warren Air Force Base, Ayden craned his neck to watch the jets slicing through the sky, their engines roaring. The military escort guided them safely through the city to the western outskirts, where they were allowed to proceed on their own.

"Stay safe, and good luck in Farson." The lead soldier waved and turned back toward the city.

With Cheyenne behind them, Ayden felt a mix of relief and trepidation. The road to Farson was still long, and the news from the corporal weighed on his mind.

Ayden's heart leaped at the sight of White Mountain's peaks. By the time they reached Rock Springs, Wyoming, intending to skirt the city and head north to Farson, it was mid-morning. They were so close that Ayden had begun to get butterflies in his stomach, looking forward to his reunion with Mia. He recalled fun times exploring the White Mountain Petroglyphs and in the high-desert sand boarding at Killpecker Sand Dunes, just a few miles north of town, which were the largest in North America and the second largest in the world, and taking the boys to explore Boar's Tusk, a long-extinct volcanic core standing above the dunes. Reflecting back, those were the absolute happiest times in his life—because Mia and the boys filled those memories with laughter and love.

A smile spread across his face as he turned onto Highway 191, pointing the Ford toward Farson. Just past the Renegade Café, a woman raced into the roadway in front of them, waving her hands over her head. Ayden slammed on his brakes and skidded to a stop in front of her. She never even flinched.

"Please!" she cried as she raced around to the driver's side. "Please! You have to help me!" She was breathless as if she'd been running a while. She took a second to catch her breath.

At his side, Laney shifted, lifting her pistol. Beside her, Mueller had turned toward the right side of the road and the café's parking lot.

"Ayden! Be careful!" he urged.

"Please! I need help. My family…" She looked Ayden in the eyes.

He could see the agony in her gaze.

"They've taken everyone!" She collapsed against the driver's door. Her hands gripped the window opening. Her knuckles were bloody and scraped as if she'd been in a fistfight. "The Russians—they took them. We have to save them—we have to save my girls."

"The Russians took your daughters?" Laney asked, lowering her pistol.

"They took everyone…" She drew out the word. "The whole town!"

Ayden's stomach sank. A knot formed in his throat. Rock Springs was only forty miles north, and the Russians had been there.

"The entire town? Where?" Laney asked.

"To Lander. To the camps in Lander."

"The whole town?" Ayden asked in disbelief.

"Not exactly. They left their collaborators and a few guards. They rolled into town during Market Days and rounded up everyone. Interrogated them. Killed a bunch. They kept everyone over at the National Guard base until yesterday. They brought in buses and took them away to that wind farm in Lander."

"How do you know they took them to the wind farm?"

"I got it from one of the collaborators, former councilman Marks. He was no good from the get-go. He said they had set up some kind of camp there to process them before sending them somewhere else, but he didn't know where."

"Have you heard anything about Farson? Have they struck there?"

"Farson? I don't know. I know there were several people from Farson here attending Market Days. Christiansen Ranch brought—"

Ayden's heart sank. "Someone from the Christiansen ranch in Farson came here?"

"Yes. They were the first ones put on the buses."

"We have to go!" Ayden put the truck into gear.

"Please! Don't leave me here!" the woman pleaded.

"Hop in!" Billie Jean dropped the tailgate and helped her up.

Laney placed her hand on his shoulder as Ayden stomped the gas, racing away. "That doesn't mean Mia was with them. Couldn't it have been some of the people who work for them? You said they had a bunch of ranch hands."

Ayden gripped the steering wheel tight. "We have to get there quick. If Mia's not at the ranch, I have to go to Lander to find her."

THIRTY

Ayden

Renegade Café
Rock Springs, Wyoming
Day Twenty-Five

The landscape was a blur as Ayden pushed the Ford to its limit, racing north along Wyoming's Highway 191 to reach Farson. Thoughts of Mia and the kids in the hands of the Russians tormented him. It was as if his worst fears were coming true. Sweat dripped from his brow as he imagined their torture and death.

It can't end like this. I can't have made it this far to lose them now!

With the gas pedal on the floor and the speedometer pegged, he willed the truck to go faster.

They flew through the tiny town of Eden, past the trailer home he'd rented with his dog Beau, and finally turned into the driveway and through the gate to the Christiansen's Ranch, where Mia's family had turned the sagebrush desert into alfalfa fields and grazed hundreds of head of cattle for over a century.

Followed by a dust cloud, he fishtailed down the gravel drive and skidded to a stop outside the Christiansens's large, two-story log home. The door flew open, and their neighbor, Helen, ran out onto the porch.

"Ayden!" she called with shock evident on her face.

"Where's Mia?" he yelled as he flung open the truck's door. "Where are the boys?"

"Everyone went to Rock Springs for Market Day!"

"They're at the wind farm," said the woman they'd picked up in Rock Springs.

Ayden's knees nearly buckled. His heart was thudding so hard in his chest he thought he might be having a heart attack.

"Monica, get everyone inside. Ayden and I are going after them!" Mueller shouted from his open door. He stepped out and moved toward the tailgate to assist her. There, he argued with his wife.

Monica pleaded with him. "You can't go! You were shot and blown up twice. Tyson, you're not strong enough!"

"We didn't come all this way for Ayden to lose his girl now. Get everyone inside. We're going to that wind farm to check it out. If we can rescue them, we'll do that."

"I'm coming with you." Laney reached into the bed of the truck and retrieved her rifle.

"Are you going to let her do that?" Monica asked.

Mueller put both of his hands on his daughter's arms. "It's too dangerous, Laney. Stay here. Help your mother."

"No way. I'm coming. Ayden helped me reunite with my family, and now I'm going to return the favor."

"See!" Monica said. "She has your stubbornness. I'm coming, too!"

"I gotta go!" Ayden entreated, his voice raised.

Finn, who had just reached the steps of the porch, turned back and ran to him. "I hope you find your girlfriend. I'd like to meet her sons."

Ayden kneeled to embrace him. "Thank you, Finn. Stay close to your grandma. I'll be back soon."

Gunner edged his nose under Ayden's arm and licked his face. Ayden heard barking coming from inside the cabin, and an instant later, his border collie, Beau Dacious, bound down the porch steps. Finn stepped back just as Beau leaped into Ayden's arms. Tears filled Ayden's eyes as he stroked his furry best friend's fur. "I missed you so much, boy. Beau whined, wagging his tail. "I have to go get Mia and the boys, and then I'll come back, and we'll play the longest game of fetch ever. Ayden stood, and Beau ran circles around him. Gunner joined him, and then the two dogs ran off, barking. "Play nice, Beau," Ayden called after him.

"They'll be good," Finn said.

"They'll be good," Finn said.

Serenity waved to Ayden as Finn ran back to the house. "Good luck! Be safe!"

Ayden nodded and then returned to the truck and climbed behind the wheel.

Without another word, Laney ran around to the passenger side and slid into the front seat, slamming the door. "Let's go!"

As Ayden put the truck into Reverse, both back doors opened, and then Monica and Mueller got in.

"How far is it to Lander?" Mueller asked.

"An hour."

THIRTY-ONE

Ayden

Red Canyon Road
Lander, Wyoming
Day Twenty-Five

Ten miles from the Sagebrush Prairie Wind Farm, Ayden steered the truck onto the dirt road that led north into Red Canyon. Trying not to lose control, he navigated near the brim of the canyon, past the Nature Conservancy's Red Canyon Ranch and Education Center. He pulled to a stop behind a cluster of pinyon-juniper woodlands, jumped out, and grabbed his backpack and rifle.

"We'll have to walk from here." He met Mueller at the front of the Ford. "I'll understand if you can't."

"The word 'can't' isn't in my vocabulary, son. Just point the way. I may have to drag my butt there, but I'll make it," Mueller said as Monica assisted him with putting his arms through the straps of his pack.

Ayden checked the ammunition in his rifle and pistol as Laney and Monica put on their backpacks and grabbed their own weapons.

"Let's do this!" Laney moved along beside him.

"Hold on," Mueller said. He reached into the bed of the truck, unlatched Frank's Pelican case, and extracted Frank's lightweight grenade launcher. Laney grabbed the six-pack 40 mm grenade pouch.

"You want me to carry that for you?" she asked.

"Just help me get the sling over my head."

Armed with the grenade launcher and all the rifle and pistol ammunition they had left, Ayden led them east toward the highway. They stopped briefly to survey the road to ensure no soldiers patrolled it. Not seeing any, they crossed over and followed the Little Popo Agie River north, past pinyon pines and junipers along draws and peaks of the high desert. From one of the ridges, they could see the expanse of wind turbines, their fiberglass blades at a standstill, having not yet been brought online. Now, Ayden imagined they would never produce electricity. They moved down the ridge for a better view of the chain-link fenced-in area.

Ayden gasped at the sight before them. An entire field, many acres wide, was filled with military vehicles, mostly cargo and transport trucks. But that wasn't the most shocking thing. It was the older couple and the small children beside them, kneeling on the pavement with guns pointed at their heads.

"We have to do something!" Laney said. "We cannot let this happen. They're just children."

Mueller already had his binoculars out and was scanning the camp. "There's too many guards. They've even got artillery down there." He pointed to the wooden guard tower. "Snipers."

Ayden's eyes stopped at the tower across the field from it. Two more Russian guards with automatic rifles stood watch over rows and rows of tents. Piles of charred and twisted metal of what might have once been construction trailers lay next to huge earthmovers and mangled cranes used to lift the giant turbines into place on their concrete foundations.

"There's a bunker—or what is left of one," Mueller said,

handing Ayden the binoculars. "See that large concrete box-looking structure on top of that mound of dirt in the middle of the fenced area?"

Ayden scanned until he located what Mueller was describing. "Yes. I found it."

"Down the hill from that are two concrete retaining walls. That's where the doors were. Now, it is just a black hole after it's been blasted open. See the char marks on the walls?"

"Yes. So the rumors were correct. They were building a survival bunker up here."

"Looks like it. Pretty dang large one judging from all those vents."

Ayden moved from the boulder to the cluster of junipers to get a better look. Russian guards were stringing three rows of concertina wire atop a fence surrounding more rows of military-style tents.

"We need to get closer and see what kind of firepower and equipment they've got guarding the camp," Mueller said.

Ayden and the Muellers crept closer, at times having to cross the open field to a new clump of trees. They managed to get within a few hundred yards of the camp but eventually ran out of natural cover. Guards walked the exterior of the fence line, patrolling the area, but Ayden saw none near the row of construction equipment.

"We have to cross here. Follow me to that excavator." Mueller gestured to the closest of the oversized pieces of machinery in a long row of construction equipment.

They followed him, dropping beside a huge tire and peering around the front of the vehicle.

"That guard is manning a 9M133 Kornet anti-tank missile," Mueller whispered. He gestured to a row of tracked vehicles. "And that there is a Pantsir—that's their air defense system. That can take out those jets from Warren Air Force Base."

"How'd they get those here already, Dad?" Laney whispered, kneeling beside them.

"No idea. Airdrop, maybe?"

"I said walk faster," a guard yelled over the hum of generators.

Ayden rose to a crouch, ran to another row of construction trucks, and dropped to his knees. Laney came up beside him, and they crawled around to the rear of the vehicle together.

"Where are they taking them?" she asked, craning her neck, trying to get a view of the soldiers and their prisoners.

"To that large tent in the middle, I think," Mueller said, moving up behind them.

The soldiers were leading the older couple and the children down the aisle between a row of tents. Among the frail-looking elderly couple and the young children were three younger men. They'd put up a fight, judging by the blood covering their faces. They walked behind another older adult couple with their shoulders slumped as if they knew their fate. If they survived this, what would become of them? Would they be sent to reeducation camps or work camps? Ayden wondered.

One of the men glanced up, and Ayden recognized him. It was Dirk, the manager of Mia's ranch. He looked like he'd taken a beating. The big guy was hunched over, his face battered and swollen, but Ayden would have recognized that mop of red hair and oversized rodeo belt buckle anywhere.

"That guy there works for Mia's dad," Ayden muttered.

"Looks like they worked him over pretty good," Mueller said.

Laney nodded. "But he's still standing."

"He's as tough as they come," Ayden said.

"What's the plan here, Dad?"

"We can't just storm the gate and free them!" Ayden exclaimed. "How can we get them out of there?"

"No, we can't do that. It would just get everyone killed. We have to be smart. Make a plan," Mueller said.

Monica protested. "No! We can't do this alone. We need help. This is a job for the military."

Ayden rubbed his face. He just wanted to storm the place and get Mia and her family out. The lack of sleep was clouding his judgment, but Monica was right. It would take a special force team or maybe an entire battalion of soldiers to rescue those prisoners. The four of them couldn't take on all those guards with the weapons they had. "I get that, but we're all they have. We have to do something."

A woman screamed, followed by the wailing of a child. Ayden spun around to find a soldier carrying a small child tucked under one arm and leading a zip-tied woman with the other. He recognized her immediately.

Mia!

"That's Mia!" Ayden said, rising from his crouch.

"No!" Mueller grabbed his arm. "You'll get her killed."

Another guard appeared, and behind him were a man and a woman, both handcuffed.

"Neil! Melody!" Ayden whispered. "That's Mia's parents."

A moment later, another soldier escorted Carter and Luke out of the tent. A second soldier walked behind them with his rifle trained on their backs.

"Those are her boys!" Ayden was filled with rage. He'd never felt so helpless in all his life. He balled his fists and worked his jaw. He wanted to open fire and mow down all the bad guys, but anger wouldn't save Mia, the boys, and her parents. He had to rein that in and be smart, like Mueller said.

"At least now you know they're alive," Mueller said.

"Where are they taking them?" Monica asked.

Mueller moved down the row of vehicles, and Ayden and others followed. Mia, her family, and the other prisoners were taken to the newly fenced area. They were shoved through a gate where more prisoners milled about. One of the male prisoners ran toward the gate. The guards stopped him, knocking him to the ground, one hitting him over the head repeatedly with the stock of his rifle.

"We can't just let this happen, guys. We have to do something."

"We will, Laney. Let me think," Mueller said. "We're going to need all the information we can get about the number of guards, their weapons, and what communications equipment they have to call for backup. Even if we get all those folks freed, it won't do any good if Russian reinforcements arrive before we kill everyone and escape."

"We don't want that," Laney said.

"No, we don't," a rough voice said behind them.

Ayden spun and fell back against one of the trucks as four US soldiers appeared out of nowhere.

The muscle-bound soldier put his finger to his lips to silence Ayden. "Sorry! Didn't mean to startle you. We had to stop you before you guys screwed up our op."

"Your operation? Are you here to rescue them?" Laney asked as she moved around her father to approach them.

"The prisoners?" the soldier asked. "Eventually. We're a recon team."

Another soldier, a man with wire-rimmed glasses and a thin build, spoke into a handheld radio. "Eight Rashist in four watchtowers."

While he continued listing off vehicles and weapons he'd observed, the first soldier introduced his team.

"I'm Sergeant First Class Shane Deminski. Those two are my weapons sergeants, Osgood and Knebel. The geeky guy on the radio is Terrance Hoehn, our communications specialist."

"Are you special forces?" Ayden asked.

Osgood chuckled. "We're pretty special, all right. We were assigned to the wind farm—before Spetsnaz seized control of it."

"Joke's on them," Knebel said, his voice a hoarse whisper. "We blew it all to shit before they got here. You should have seen all those rich boys running out in their silk PJs screaming like little girls."

"What's the plan, Deminski?" Mueller asked.

"Observe. Report."

"And then what?" Ayden snapped. "My girlfriend and her family are down there. I need to know what you plan to do to get them out—safely!"

"We know. Our team was staying at the Christiansens's ranch when they were captured. We're as anxious as you are to get them out, but we have to follow orders, observe, and let headquarters run the raid to free them."

"How long will that take?"

Knebel shifted position to the next vehicle, then glanced back over his shoulder at Hoehn.

"As soon as the rest of our snipers move into place," Hoehn said. "They're just about there."

"I got to say. You four are pretty damn lucky," Deminski said. "If Knebel hadn't called out that you were Americans, you'd be toast right now. Overwatch would have smoked you on your way in."

"Yeah, we watched you approach," Osgood said. "There was some debate about dropping you anyway, so you didn't blow our operation." He smiled over at Knebel. "But Knebel said—"

Knebel shot him a look. "Can it, Osgood. We came down here to keep you from getting yourselves killed."

"We need you to follow us out of the area," Deminski said, gesturing back the way Ayden and the others came in.

"You have enough soldiers here to rescue them?" Ayden asked as he turned to follow Osgood.

"Four teams. Eighteen operators. Bravo, Charlie, and Delta are moving into place. Once they arrive at their checkpoint, they'll neutralize the guard force and prepare to blow up these missile systems. When we get the prisoners out, the birds can come in and take out the bunker before they rebuild it and dig themselves in like ticks."

Ayden and the Muellers followed the soldiers back to the outskirts of the wind farm. As he approached a slight rise in the hill, Ayden looked back just as one of the teams began to pour through a hole in the perimeter fence.

"Keep moving!" Osgood barked, waving them on.

They moved over the next rise and came across four US soldiers who were doing their best to hold their position against more than ten Russians.

Raising his rifle to his shoulder as he ran toward them, Osgood squeezed off rounds at full auto. Russian soldiers started dropping left and right. Within moments, they had neutralized all ten enemy fighters and were moving toward the camp.

Ayden held his breath for a moment as the teams advanced toward the fence line. Somewhere in the hills, snipers cleared a path for them as they crept through the sagebrush and past clusters of junipers. They stopped every so often to allow the snipers to eliminate targets.

"Go, you two! Go! I'll cover you!" Osgood yelled.

Ayden didn't move. He couldn't. He needed to watch them rescue Mia.

Suddenly, rounds kicked up dirt near Ayden's feet. Russian soldiers poured over the rise, firing at them.

"Run!" Osgood shouted, returning fire. "Get to that wash!"

THIRTY-TWO

Ayden

Sagebrush Prairie Wind Farm
Fremont County, Wyoming
Day Twenty-Five

As Russian soldiers poured over the rise, Ayden began firing, emptying his magazine as he ran toward the ravine. He dove into the wash beside Laney, who'd reached it first. She popped up and fired, covering her mother and father as they ran toward them.

Ayden dropped his spent magazine, slapped a new one into place, and hit the bolt release. "Hurry!" he shouted to Mueller.

"Run, Daddy!" Laney screamed.

One of the US soldiers who had been running just behind them dropped down to a knee and fired off a string of automatic rifle rounds. He cut down a dozen or more Russians who were nearly on top of them.

Several other US soldiers ran up behind them, dropping into the ravine, opening fire on the attackers and quickly ripping the remaining Russian soldiers apart.

In the distance, artillery guns inside the camp fired at some unseen target.

Osgood jumped up, barked obscenity-laden orders to the US soldiers, and they hopped up and took off toward the camp. "Form up and follow me!" he ordered.

Zip, zap.

Bullets flew in their direction, kicking up dust and hitting juniper trees and sagebrush around them. One of the guard towers not far from them had let loose on their positions. "Take that tower out!" shouted Osgood.

One of the soldiers dropped to his knees and fumbled with the latch on a large metal box, then shouldered a grenade gun, aiming it at the tower.

Pop...bam.

The grenade hit the tower, and within seconds, the tower flew apart into splinters.

By that time, more than two dozen Russian soldiers had started flooding into the grounds from inside the bunker. Immediately, they began firing back at their position.

Mueller handed Frank's grenade launcher to Osgood. Laney dropped the pouch of grenades at his feet. He shouldered it and launched grenade after grenade until the pouch was empty.

One of Osgood's soldiers took a hit, tumbled, and landed face-first in the dirt.

Another was struck in the leg, and then another fell, crying out in agony.

Ayden, Laney, Mueller, and Monica joined in the fight, firing their rifles at the Russians. A cascade of debris showered Ayden, kicked up by the rounds, repeatedly striking the boulder they had taken cover behind. When the cloud had dissipated enough for him to see again, he rose up on his right knee and brought his rifle to bear. Ahead of him, only a handful of enemy soldiers remained in the fight.

"Contact front!" the point man shouted. Then the entire world in front of them erupted in gunfire as more Russian soldiers poured from the bunker.

"Get down!" someone yelled.

Crack, crack, boom!

Bullets flew back and forth between the two groups, and a chorus of orders and angry shouts echoed throughout the field.

Osgood took a knee next to one of the pine trees. They were outnumbered, and all around them, grenades were going off. It was clear the Russians were going to overwhelm them. Not only was he unable to rescue Mia and her boys, but he was also facing the grim fate of dying right there in the dirt.

Up ahead, a sudden fireball turned dusk into daylight. The distinct sound of a fighter jet roared overhead. Had help arrived for them—or for the Russians? A few seconds later, four attack helicopters flew over. Following more explosions, the battlefield grew silent, except for the cries of the wounded.

Ayden jumped up and ran toward the camp. He rounded the construction vehicles just as a US soldier was leading the prisoners from the camp to the roadway in front of the wind farm. He sprinted after them. His breath hitched as he spotted Mia in the crowd. His hand flew up as he called her name.

"Mia! Mia! Oh my God! Mia!"

Her head rotated toward him, and he gasped at the sight of the bruises on her face. Mia's eyes widened with recognition, and she said something he couldn't hear.

Ayden weaved between survivors and raced to Mia, wrapped her in his arms and lifted her small frame off the ground. He spun her around as he repeatedly kissed her cheek over and over.

"Ayden!" Mia cried, tears streaming down her cheeks. "You—"

He kissed her lips and held her tight.

"You're here? You're really here!"

"I'm here, my love. I'm here, and you're safe now!" He held her tight.

"Ayden!" Xavy screamed.

Ayden looked over Mia's shoulder to find all three of her boys running toward them. He took a step back. Facing them, he dropped to his knees with his arms flung open wide. Carter was the first to reach him.

Losing it, Ayden broke into sobs, cradling the boy.

"Ayden! Ayden!" Luke cried as he dove into his arms, wrapping his arms around Ayden's neck so tight that Ayden couldn't breathe.

Behind him, Xavier stopped short.

Ayden reached for him. "Xavy!"

Xavier leaped and piled on top of his brothers. The four of them rolled around, laughing as Ayden tickled each boy. Carter jumped on Ayden's back, and the two rolled until Ayden was face up on the ground with all three of the boys' bony fingers poking his sides and belly.

Playing with those kids was the best moment of Ayden's entire life and everything he'd dreamed of for the last three weeks.

"Okay, boys!" Mia's father, Neil, stood over them. "Let him catch his breath."

The boys rolled off and lay beside him. Ayden started to roll over to get to his feet, when Mia dropped beside them, and the tickle melee began again.

After a few minutes, Ayden came out on top.

"I surrender! I surrender!" Mia laughed and cried at the same time.

"This is fun to watch and all, but we need to go unless you want to walk all the way back to the ranch," Deminski said, standing over them.

"I've had enough of walking." Mueller held his injured left arm against his abdomen.

Monica and Laney rushed to his side, and each wrapped their arms around him, assisting him toward the awaiting buses—the same ones the Russians had used to transport the prisoners there.

While Melody, Mia's mother, was guiding the boys toward the

bus, Mia and Ayden positioned themselves next to a newly arrived Humvee.

"Are you okay?" Ayden asked, touching his palm to her cheek. It was so amazing to be staring into her eyes again that his heart could barely take it.

She pressed her body against his and wrapped her arms around his waist. With her head on his chest, she looked up at him. "I am now that you've made it home!"

He kissed the top of her head and stared off, watching the boys climb onto the bus that would take them all back to the ranch. He was home. His heart was home—with Mia and the boys, and no matter what, he vowed he'd never leave them again.

Ayden reached into his pocket and palmed his mother's ring, which he'd carried with him all the way from Manhattan. He swallowed hard and held his hand out to her.

Mia smiled. "What do you have there?"

"My promise."

She looked at him, questioning. "Your promise?"

Ayden dropped to one knee before Mia and took her hand in his.

"Ayden!" Tears glistened in Mia's eyes.

"Mia Adelaide Christiansen." He smiled up at her and held the ring out. "With all my heart, I promise to be the unwavering guide who will lead you out of the shadows, a constant source of warmth that provides solace even in the coldest of times, and a steady shoulder for you to lean on when life becomes too overwhelming to bear on your own. Will you marry me?"

"Say yes!" Osgood shouted from the door of the bus.

Mia glanced back over her shoulder.

"Say yes, so we can get back to the ranch and cook some steaks!"

She returned her gaze to Ayden and nodded. Tears filled her eyes. "Yes! Yes! Yes!"

Thank you for reading **Desolation**, the fourth installment of the heart-pounding *Conquer the Dark* series. The journey of Ayden, Mia, Serenity, and the others continues in **Resistance**, book five of the series—coming soon! Click here or go to Amazon.com to pre-order your copy today.

As you eagerly anticipate the next chapter in their saga, immerse yourself in the captivating world of Endure the Dark, the inaugural novel of the companion series *Reign of Darkness*. This foundational book lays the groundwork for the epic adventures to come, introducing you to characters whose destinies have intertwined with Ayden's and Mia's in unforeseen ways.

Keep scrolling to read a sample of *Endure the Dark: Reign of Darkness, Book One*. **Don't forget to sign up for my spam-free newsletter today and receive a FREE copy of Finn and Gunner's story, Last Light: A Reign of Darkness Novella and be the first to know of new releases, giveaways, and special offers.**

Sample of Endure the Dark

REIGN OF DARKNESS SERIES BOOK ONE

CHAPTER ONE
Serenity Jones

Main Street
Dentonville, Pennsylvania
One Week before Event

From the corner of her eye, Serenity Jones noticed two male silhouettes advancing parallel to her on the other side of Main Street. An icy shiver ran down her spine as she clenched the straps of her backpack and picked up her pace. Instead of risking a direct glance at the men, she flicked her eyes toward the reflective surface of a storefront window she was passing. It gave her the opportunity to scrutinize the figures trailing her, under the pretense of casual window shopping.

As soon as she saw their faces, she recognized her pursuers. It was them. It was the two men from the corner where she'd spent the afternoon panhandling. They'd argued with her over the spot she'd claimed as her own for the last two years, ever since she had first come to live on the streets at the age of fourteen.

A knot of dread twisted in her stomach. Had they followed her? They were like predators on the prowl, mirroring her steps across the street.

One of them glanced in her direction before pointing toward an alleyway on her side of the street. Then, like they were in sync, they both walked toward her, their intent apparent in their intimidating strides. Were they plotting to corner her in that deserted alley?

As soon as the men vanished around the building's corner, Serenity seized her chance. She darted across the street and slipped into the comforting refuge of Harrington's Bistro. Shrugging off her backpack, she let it thud onto a booth seat by the window and slid in after it. In a swift motion, she picked up a menu from the table rack and used it as a veil to blend into the restaurant's ambiance while keeping her eyes peeled on the street outside.

Instinctively, she reached into her pocket, expecting to feel the ironwood handle of her pocketknife, and then remembered it was still tucked securely beneath her sleeping pad back at her tent. An uncomfortable vulnerability gnawed at her as she registered its absence. She had left the knife behind that morning, knowing that carrying weapons was strictly forbidden at the youth shelter she frequented for an occasional, much-needed shower and to get clean clothes.

The knife had been a gift from her father, a relic from a time when safety wasn't a daily struggle. It had been her constant companion since she'd been living on the streets, and now, more than ever, she felt vulnerable and exposed without it.

Serenity chanced a peek over the top of the menu, her gaze trained on the alley from where she expected the pair to emerge. And emerge they did. The taller figure cast wary glances into the store windows as if hunting for her, while the shorter one ripped open the door of the neighboring hair salon.

Every nerve in Serenity's body was on high alert. As usual, she was already strategizing and plotting her next two moves to maneuver out of this dangerous predicament. They were looking for her. That was obvious. It was a deadly game of hide and seek, and they'd aimed to make her their prey—their mistake!

"Are you going to order something?" The question hurled at her sliced through the tense silence with a sharp-edged hostility. The voice belonged to the waitress, a woman who had long since abandoned any pretense of hospitality. Her deep-set eyes, with deep crow's-feet webbing from the corners, were filled with fatigue and frustration. She wore her blonde hair pulled back into a taut ponytail, the severe style exacerbating her perpetual scowl. Her impatience and disinterest seemed as ingrained as the coffee stains on her apron.

Harrington's bistro had a tired appearance, just like the people in it. Tucked away in a quieter corner of the city, its once-polished mahogany furniture now looked muted and scratched. Faded tapestries lined the walls, their lack of color testifying to many a day spent under the harsh sunlight. There was some great jazz playing on a crappy stereo in the restaurant, but you could barely hear it over the sounds of people talking. It was a haven for the likes of Serenity—a little run-down, somewhat invisible, but still enduring.

Serenity gave the waitress a side-on look, trying to play it cool. "Just a water, please."

"You gotta order food or pay for a drink," she said firmly.

The delicious aroma wafting from the kitchen taunted Serenity's empty stomach. She cast a longing glance at the menu and the mouth-watering images of juicy hamburgers, cheesy pizzas—even the golden-brown grilled cheese sandwich stirred a visceral hunger. If only she could...

"Water is a drink."

"We charge for it," the waitress fired back, scowling.

Serenity shrugged. She rose from the booth, the worn vinyl squeaking in protest, and passed the menu back. "Fine." Her voice dropped into a conspiratorial whisper. "You got a back door here?"

The waitress's sharp eyes followed her gaze across the bustling street. Her tone softened. "Those guys giving you trouble?"

Serenity offered a slight nod in response without taking her eyes off the men, who seemed increasingly agitated.

"Through the kitchen." The waitress gestured with a nod toward the back of the bistro. "There's a door that leads straight to the alley."

Serenity's eyes flickered with gratitude. "Appreciate it," she replied, her voice barely more than a whisper.

Serenity's sneakers scraped against the checkerboard floor as she navigated through the bistro toward the kitchen, a ripple of attention following in her wake. The hum of chitchat among white-collar workers on their lunch break stuttered, their gazes slicing through the air to land on her. City shoppers with their nice clothes and polished shoes gave her the once over and then wrinkled their noses as if they'd caught a whiff of something unpleasant. Those looks—a mix of disdain and poorly concealed pity—felt like cold daggers scraping against the thin walls of her pride. She could almost hear the whispers behind manicured hands, their pointed fingers masked behind expensive designer bags. Yet Serenity bore it all with a hardened exterior, an armor forged on the unforgiving streets. No matter what they thought, they were no better than her. Her eyes, lit by the fire of gritty resolve, remained locked ahead. Such glances were the price for staying alive and being free. And no one could rob her of that freedom.

The kitchen was a cacophony of smells and sounds. The sizzle and spit of meat on hot grills, the rhythmic chop-chop of sharp knives against wooden boards, and the symphony of clanging pots and pans all merged into a chaotic harmony. The air was heavy with the aroma of grilled meat, simmering sauces, and the pungent scent of spices, creating a sensory tapestry that was both over-whelming and oddly comforting.

The cook, a burly man with a generous belly spilling over his apron and sweat glistening on his brow, halted mid-stir as he noticed her. His bushy eyebrows shot up in surprise, a wooden spoon dripping with thick red sauce suspended in midair. His graying hair and weary, weathered face spoke of a hectic life lived in the unforgiving crucible of kitchen heat.

Serenity caught the faint traces of worry etched into the lines of his face as if he were a man hanging onto the fringes of stability, treading the thin line between a warm bed and the unrelenting hardness of the sidewalk. It was a reality she knew only too well; the city was littered with stories of lives that had derailed, of people who were only one missed paycheck away from where she was now.

She offered him a curt nod, an unspoken acknowledgment of the shared understanding that existed between them. Their lives might have been worlds apart, but in the grand scheme of things, they were both just survivors, fighting to make it another day in the ruthless jungle of urban life.

Once outside, the back alley greeted her in stark contrast to the frenzy of the kitchen. The smell of stale garbage and cigarettes hung heavy in the air, an unsavory mix that was a far cry from the rich and tempting aromas she'd just left behind. A figure appeared within the darkness, the glowing end of a cigarette briefly showing his gaunt face. She locked eyes with the kitchen worker as he threw away his cigarette, the embers fizzling out on the wet ground.

Turning from her, he pulled a bulging garbage bag from the bin, the metallic scrape echoing through the alley. Serenity tightened the straps of her backpack and then twisted her long, blonde hair into a ponytail and secured it with a hair tie. As he tossed the bag into the dumpster, Serenity bolted. Her sneakers pounded against the grimy concrete as she raced north, past the backs of the buildings of Main Street in a blur. Her heart hammered in her chest, adrenaline fueling her every stride. She didn't stop until she'd reached the end of the row, where the narrow alley spat her out onto Gallagher Street.

Serenity paused, gasping for breath as she took in her surroundings, her eyes darting for any sign of the men who'd pursued her. She was safe for the moment in the bustling streets of Dentonville, Pennsylvania. The city continued to live and breathe around her, oblivious and uncaring.

With the gritty brick facade of Gallagher Title and Escrow firm at her back, she cautiously risked a look around its corner. She breathed a sigh of relief when she saw the coast was clear. She launched herself forward and darted across Gallagher Street, dodging through sparse traffic. Confident she'd shaken her pursuers, Serenity turned south, toward the more run-down part of town, the derelict Gallagher Bank, and the patch of neglected ground nearby that she called home.

At the intersection of Elgin Avenue and Freeport Street, the sounds of city life hummed along with the occasional horn honking or sirens in the distance. Here, Serenity allowed her pace to ease to a slow walk. The knot of tension that had been winding tighter and tighter within her began to uncoil.

Passing by the bakery, the smell of freshly baked bread caused her stomach to growl. She stopped for a moment to glance into the shop's window. The pastries looked like little slices of heaven. She shoved her hand inside her pocket. She'd made two dollars and twenty-five cents before those a-holes ran her off from her most lucrative panhandling spot.

Suddenly, the door to the neighboring flower shop swung open to reveal the face of a little boy. "Finn! Wait for Mommy," a woman's voice admonished from inside.

Finn grinned at Serenity, taking a step onto the sidewalk, followed by a black and tan beagle dog. "Mom says the brioche here's top-notch, but I swear by Mrs. Hughes's pastéis de nata. They've got this wild story—monks, leftover egg yolks, and an old sugar refinery turning it into a bakery hit in the 1800s."

Serenity's mouth dropped open. She couldn't believe such a

young kid could even pronounce pastéis de nata, let alone know who invented them. "How old are you, kid?" Serenity asked.

"I'm six years old. I will be seven on October 13. Grandma Jane is taking me on a tour of the Center for Nanotechnology for my birthday."

The boy's dog made a circle around Serenity, sniffing her jeans and sneakers. He stopped in front of her and nudged his nose under her hand. She petted the dog's head and said, "That sounds interesting."

Finn nodded.

"So you like science?"

"I'm an inventor, so of course I'm interested in science and technology. I also enjoy music—mostly blues and some classic rock."

Serenity chuckled at the range of his musical interest.

The kid took two steps forward and thrust out his hand. "I'm Finn, and this is my dog, Gunner."

Serenity glanced around, expecting the kid's parents to run up and pull him away from her. Yet Finn just stood there with his hand extended, clearly waiting for her to take it. Serenity shook his hand and took a giant step back—just in case. She didn't want to be accused of trying to snatch him or something. "I'm Serenity."

"Are you homeless?" Finn asked in that frank, nonjudgmental way young kids often did.

"Yes."

"Where do you sleep?"

"In a tent, behind a factory."

His expression changed from a curious look to one of sadness. The dog moved his head from side to side, staring at the boy, and then he rose and walked back to him.

"My parents got divorced. My mom and I got to keep the house." The kid's expression brightened. "My mom owns the flower shop. I come here after school."

Serenity glanced next door and smiled. "Must be a nice place to do your homework—surrounded by all the pretty flowers."

"I don't have homework. I get all my assignments completed at school. I do study here at the shop, though—and read. I love books.

"I'm currently in the second grade, but I'll advance to the fourth grade in the fall. I read at a fifth-grade level, but Grandma Jane helps me pick out middle-grade books every Saturday."

A memory fluttered through Serenity's mind. Her grandmother had bought her a new book every week—until her heart attack. The books were always of a different genre. Gram had wanted to expose Serenity to a wide range of books so she'd know what she enjoyed reading most.

Serenity heard a bell jingle. Gunner bolted inside through the open door as a woman in her early thirties stepped out. "Finn! What have I told you about talking to strangers?"

"She's not a stranger, Mom. This is Serenity. She lives in a tent."

"I'm sorry. He likes people." Finn's mom grabbed his hand and pulled him back toward the flower shop.

Finn waved goodbye before the door closed behind them. Serenity crossed the street, glanced back at the flower shop one last time, and then turned the corner and entered the alley.

She was safe, for now, and that was all that mattered. As she walked toward her tent, the muted sounds of Dentonville served as a somber soundtrack to the end of her day. The struggles of survival were a constant companion. They were nothing new. She'd been fighting the battle all her life. Today, like many days before, she had won.

Just as she was allowing her thoughts to drift toward the comfort of her tent and the remaining chapters of her worn, secondhand novel, a figure sprang into her path, jolting her back into reality.

~

CHAPTER TWO
Keith Jones

State Correctional Institution (SCI) Green
Waynesburg, Pennsylvania
One Week before Event

A prison cell had become Keith Jones's world. The metal bars, the dull colors, and the constant chatter of other inmates, along with the cold, sterile hallways, served as a daily reminder of his bad choices. The corridor's dim, flickering fluorescent light made Keith's surroundings feel even more oppressive. He had a bad feeling in the pit of his stomach as he walked toward the showers. The cell block echoed with whispers and the shuffling of feet, but one set of footsteps sounded louder, getting closer.

Keith glanced back over his shoulder as he turned into the shower room but saw no one following him. The air in the prison shower room was thick with humidity due to constant use and inadequate ventilation; its grimy white tiles, spotted with mold, and the perpetual stench of decay and cheap disinfectant never failed to turn his stomach.

Steeling himself, Keith stepped onto the wet floor. His footfalls made a muted splash, the sound echoing slightly off the tiled walls. Above him, fluorescent lights buzzed and flickered. Rows of shower heads lined the walls, some dripping water continuously. The sound of the door creaking open again made him tense. Early that day, he'd received a tip from a fellow inmate that an attack on him was imminent. He had enemies inside the prison walls and no way to avoid trouble. Informing the guards would do nothing. Inmates handled issues like that themselves.

Another set of footsteps began to echo through the room, each step deliberate and measured. The sound grew ever louder, reverberating ominously in the closed space. Keith kept his face neutral but heightened his senses, listening intently. Without turning, he positioned himself with his back against the wall to ensure that whoever approached wouldn't catch him off guard. His pulse quickened in anticipation and uncertainty, forming a knot in his stomach.

Juan Rodriguez stepped into view and Keith stiffened. Rodriguez was a known associate to Rafe, Keith's partner in the heist that had landed him behind bars.

"Jones," Rodriguez growled, holding up a sharpened toothbrush honed to a lethal point. "Rafe wants to know where the cash is. He's tired of waiting for his money. Think this might jog your memory?"

Keith's eyes darted to the shank, then back up to Rodriguez. "I don't have it," he said in a steady voice despite the surge of adrenaline. "As I've told you all along—the cops took it."

Rodriguez scowled. "Don't play games with me! The police report says they never recovered the money."

"They did. As they led me away from my house, I saw Officer Brown pick up the duffle and carry it to his patrol car."

"Liar! I'm going to kill you if you don't tell me where you stashed the money!"

Rodriguez lunged at him. The shank made a swift arc through the mist, but Keith's instincts and agility got him out of its way. Barely. Rodriguez's speed caught him off guard, forcing Keith to react with a powerful right hook to the man's cheekbone. The impact reverberated, making Rodriguez's head snap back, his dark eyes momentarily clouded with surprise.

But Keith wasn't about to rest on a single punch. He had to incapacitate his opponent swiftly, so he raised his leg, aiming to deliver a powerful blow to Rodriguez's head. But somehow, Rodriguez jerked to the side and latched on to Keith's foot, causing him to lose balance and crash onto the wet tiles.

Rodriguez towered over him, silhouetted in the shower's

diffused light, ready to plunge the shank into his torso. Summoning all his strength, Keith delivered a swift kick to Rodriguez's knee, bringing him down momentarily. Then Keith sprang up and readied himself to defend or strike as the situation demanded. Now, it was Keith who was standing over his attacker. However, his moment of triumph was cut short by the sound of footfalls from the corridor. It could be prison guards or more inmates ready to join the fight.

In that split second of distraction, Rodriguez aimed the shank straight for Keith's heart. With a burst of adrenaline, Keith caught Rodriguez's wrist, redirected the weapon, and plunged it into Rodriguez's own chest with one swift, brutal motion.

As soon as he took a moment to breathe, a blow landed on Keith's back, knocking him down. Rodriguez's crew had joined the fight. Outnumbered and on slippery ground, Keith fought with the ferocity of a cornered beast and sent one of the attackers reeling with a punch to the throat. But the numbers game was catching up. Just as Keith was on the verge of being overwhelmed, a blaring alarm sounded, and the bright lights of the corridor were joined by the rapid footfalls of approaching guards. The inmates paused, but not for long. The guards might be coming, but Rodriguez wasn't done. From the ground, he shouted for his crew to finish what he'd started. "Get him!"

Keith was nearly at his limit, panting heavily. He managed to land a few more punches in a valiant effort to keep them at bay, while in his peripheral, he watched Rodriguez pulling the shank from his chest with a grimace of pain. Keith tried to shift out of reach, but Rodriguez managed to slice it into Keith's side. Pain seared through Keith, momentarily blinding him.

Then, like the cavalry in a war movie, guards burst into the room with their batons swinging. They quickly subdued the men, but to Keith's shock, he was the one yanked up and cuffed. "Thought you could start a brawl and get away with it, Jones?" one guard sneered, his face inches from Keith's.

Rodriguez, pale and gasping, lay in a puddle of water and blood, his fate uncertain. Keith knew if he didn't make it, he'd be facing another murder charge.

Despite his injuries, Keith was given a cursory check in the infirmary before being thrown into the cold, stark isolation of solitary confinement. And then he was alone, with just the sound of his heavy breathing and the terrifying thought of how much power Rafe had in this jail. Weighed down by guilt and regret, Keith lay in his bunk thinking about his daughter. He had thought about the day that changed their lives countless times, replaying every detail, every choice, and every mistake.

Normally, he only did heists with his own crew, which consisted of long-time friends, including his best friend, Pete, whom Serenity called uncle. However, at the last moment, the driver in Rafe's crew got popped by law enforcement. They should have shut down the job right then. The risk was too great—the guy knew too much—he could talk, and they'd all go to jail. That was Keith's second mistake. The first was agreeing to do a heist with a crew he didn't know all that well and with Rafe Thomas in charge.

That fateful morning had started routinely enough. As Keith had dropped Serenity off at school, her deep blue eyes filled with concern. "Dad, I have a bad feeling about this. Don't do it."

He'd given her a reassuring smile, trying to brush off the unease in his gut. "Everything's going to be fine, baby. Just another job." But deep down, he knew it was a lie. The stakes were higher, the crew was different, and the risk was immeasurable. Keith had always been open with Serenity about the life he led, not in a way that glorified it but in a manner that prepared her for the world he inhabited. She'd grown up knowing his crew, her "uncles" who doted on her while imparting vital survival skills. With his knack for getting into places unnoticed, Carlos taught her the delicate art of picking locks, turning the tumbler just so, feeling the mechanism give.

Pete, ever the mentor, introduced her to the sport of archery.

Keith remembered watching them in the backyard, Pete patiently correcting her stance, guiding her hand to release the string just right. Under his guidance, Serenity had not just learned but excelled. She even joined the school's archery team, and soon, her room was adorned with medals and certificates.

Serenity's words had struck a chord in Keith. She had good instincts. Her unease made Keith feel uneasy, too, since he was having doubts about the job. Pulling away from the school, Keith's thoughts were in turmoil. He dialed Pete, needing the reassurance of his long-time friend.

"Hey, it's me," he began, trying to sound casual, but the strain was evident in his voice. "Look, something came up. Rafe's driver can't make it—he got arrested for outstanding speeding tickets last night. I need you in on this, Pete. I trust you. I need someone I can rely on."

There was a brief pause on the other end. "All right," Pete replied, his voice steady. "But if Rafe's driver got popped, are you sure you want to go through with this? He could be spilling his guts to the cops as we speak."

Keith sighed. "I'm in too deep, Pete. I owe Scarface, and time's running out. But with you there, we can get in and get back out before the cops have time to even talk to the guy."

So the two friends made a plan to meet, not only sealing their fate for the day but setting in motion a series of events that would change their lives forever.

Pete was waiting when Keith got to the meeting point. "Are you sure about this, D?" Pete asked, glancing around nervously. Keith took a deep breath, reminded of his spiraling debts to Scarface. There was no choice, not really. Not when he had to protect Serenity and get out of the ruthless grip of the bookie.

"Let's just get this done," Keith said, trying to hide the dread creeping into his voice.

The plan had been simple on paper: in and out. The guy doing the money laundering for the cartel ran a lax operation. He never thought someone in Dentonville would have the balls to go after a Mexican cartel's money. He had one guard at the door, and the lock on the room where they stored the money waiting to be deposited into a bank account was easy to pick—it was too easy. From the moment they entered the laundromat, Keith felt a nagging sensation that they had underestimated this job. The unease grew ever stronger as they began to move the money.

When they made their way to the exit leading to the alley behind the laundromat and Pete's waiting car, the shrill sound of sirens cut through the morning air. Keith's heart sank. Red and blue lights flashed outside, casting a harsh light onto the unfolding scene. The getaway car was blocked in. Pete was trapped between them. Before Keith could process the situation, Rafe, eyes wild, began shooting.

Unarmed and caught off guard, Pete jumped out of the car to run, but the cops fired, and Pete took a bullet to the chest. Time seemed to slow down. Keith watched in horror as his best friend, his brother in every way but blood, crumbled to the ground. There was no time to mourn; his survival instincts kicked in. Keith and Rafe fled the scene, leaving behind chaos and betrayal.

In the days and months that followed, Keith was arrested, tried, and sentenced to life in prison—with no chance of parole. Serenity was taken away and placed in foster care. The weight of his choices crushed him. His parents moved back from Florida to fight for custody of their granddaughter. They did their best to give Serenity a semblance of normalcy. They bought a home close to the prison and frequently brought her to visit him there. Keith clung to those visits, which were a lifeline in the cold, harsh world of prison.

Keith was haunted by a particularly painful memory that played out with heartbreaking clarity against the backdrop of his mind. He remembered the prison guard approaching, a sealed letter held gingerly in his hand and a somber look painting his features. The weight of the envelope, unassuming as it was, seemed to press down heavily in Keith's trembling hands. Upon breaking the seal, the words blurred as his heart raced. His father, the anchor of his childhood, who had steadied his hand during his first bike ride and taught him how to navigate life's tumultuous seas, had been brutally taken from him. Through clandestine conversations and a few discreet police visits, Keith pieced together the horrifying puzzle.

Rafe and his crew, propelled by their insatiable greed and the misplaced conviction that Keith's father had knowledge of the stolen money's whereabouts, had launched an attack on his residence, killing his father before tossing the house. Guilt ate away at Keith. Rafe hadn't pulled the trigger, but Keith knew he was the one ultimately responsible for what had happened to his dad and his daughter, Serenity. Keith believed the stress of caring for Serenity and having a son in prison had ultimately led to his mother's heart attack. So, in reality, Rafe had killed both his parents.

The weight of his choices pressed down even harder. How had his life led to this?

In the late hours of the night, Keith had spoken to Leo, his cellmate, who was an older man with gray streaks in his hair and a calm disposition. Leo had become a father figure to Keith during their time together, and he often shared wisdom from his own tumultuous past. Leo had spent over half his life behind bars and left behind a family, too. He knew the weight of guilt that was crushing Keith.

"Leo," Keith whispered, voice choked with emotion, "My father is gone. And it's all because of me."

Leo looked up from his book and gestured for Keith to sit beside him. "Life is full of choices, son. Some we're proud of, and others we regret. But it's never too late to change."

Keith looked down, the weight of the world on his shoulders. "I want to, but I don't even know where to begin. I've hurt Serenity so much. She deserves better."

Leo placed a comforting hand on Keith's shoulder. "Begin with her. Reach out, even if it's just a letter. Let her know your regrets, your love, and your hope for her future."

Taking Leo's advice to heart, Keith began to pen letters to Serenity. He wrote of memories of the times he'd been there for her and the times he'd let her down. He shared his remorse and the lessons he had learned. Each word was filled with a father's love and hope for forgiveness. However, as weeks turned into months, without any response from his daughter, he had thought she wanted nothing more to do with him. It was as if the ground had been ripped out from beneath him. His daughter, his precious Serenity, was facing the harshest realities, all alone. The thought was unbearable. Every night that followed was sleepless, filled with anguish and guilt.

It's never too late to change, Leo had said.

Keith was determined. He would find a way to turn his life around, to right the wrongs, and most importantly, to find Serenity and get her into the home she deserved—he could think of no better use for the ill-gotten money.

Thank you for reading this sample of *Endure the Dark*, book one in the *Reign of Darkness* series, a *Conquer the Dark* companion series. Click here to order your copy and continue reading Endure the Dark today!

This foundational book lays the groundwork for the epic adventures to come, introducing you to characters whose destinies will intertwine with Ayden and Clara in unforeseen ways.

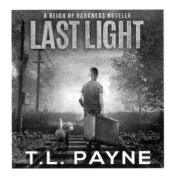

Don't forget to sign up for my spam-free newsletter today and receive a FREE copy of Last Light: A Reign of Darkness Novella and be the first to know of new releases, giveaways, and special offers.

Also by T. L. Payne

Conquer the Dark Series

A Reign of Darkness Companion Series

Collapse

Ruin

Carnage

Desolation

Resistance (Coming soon!)

Reign of Darkness Series

Endure the Dark

Escape the Destruction

Evade the Ruthless

Engage the Enemy (Pre-order Now!)

Last Light: A Reign of Darkness Novella

(Newsletter signup required)

Days of Want Series

Turbulent

Hunted

Turmoil

Uprising

Upheaval

Mayhem

Defiance

Sudden Chaos: A Post Apocalyptic EMP Survival Story

(Newsletter signup required)

Fall of Houston Series

A Days of Want Companion Series

No Way Out

No Other Choice

No Turning Back

No Surrender

No Man's Land

Gateway to Chaos Series

Seeking Safety

Seeking Refuge

Seeking Justice

Seeking Hope

Survive the Collapse Series

Brink of Darkness

Brink of Chaos

Brink of Panic

Brink of Collapse

Brink of Destruction: A FREE Novelette

Desperate Age Series

Panic in the Rockies

Getting Out of Dodge

Surviving Freedom

Trouble in Tulsa

Defending Camp

This We'll Defend: A Desperate Age Novella

(Newsletter signup required)